THE SCARLET CAR

BY
RICHARD HARDING DAVIS

Illustrated by
Frederic Dorr Steele

TO
NED STONE

CONTENTS

INTRODUCTION TO THE 100th ANNIVERSARY EDITION

The automobile was still in its infancy a hundred years ago when Richard Harding Davis wrote *The Scarlet Car*, arguably the first example of automotive fiction by a serious author. Davis was the best known war correspondent of the Spanish American War and was considered one of the top journalists of the day. He was also a popular writer of fiction, romance and drama. His work and his life influenced other writers such as Ernest Hemingway, Sinclair Lewis, Jack London and H.L. Mencken.

In *The Scarlet Car*, Davis captures the adventure and uncertainty that was a major part of travel by automobile in the early 20th century. His period prose provides just enough description of the rigors of automotive travel without bogging the reader in the details. Importantly, his short novel is about people, not machinery.

The Scarlet Car was published by Charles Scribner's Sons in 1907. Sadly, Richard Harding Davis didn't write additional stories about the automobile, and although he was an influence on other significant adventure writers, few writers since his time have followed his lead and explored the genre of automotive fiction. *The Scarlet Car* stands among the very earliest works about life and adventure with the automobile.

This edition of *The Scarlet Car* has been published by Demontreville Press, Inc., to commemorate and recognize the 100th anniversary of the beginning of automotive fiction.

Demontreville Press, Inc.
Lake Elmo, Minnesota
March, 2007

Miss Forbes

CHAPTER I
THE JAIL-BREAKERS

For a long time it had been arranged they all should go to the Harvard and Yale game in Winthrop's car. It was perfectly well understood. Even Peabody, who pictured himself and Miss Forbes in the back of the car, with her brother and Winthrop in front, condescended to approve. It was necessary to invite Peabody because it was his great good fortune to be engaged to Miss Forbes. Her brother Sam had been invited, not only because he could act as chaperon for his sister, but because since they were at St. Paul's, Winthrop and he, either as participants or spectators, had never missed going together to the Yale-Harvard game. And Beatrice Forbes herself had been invited because she was herself.

When at nine o'clock on the morning of the game, Winthrop stopped the car in front of her door. He was in love with all the world. In the November air there was a sting like frost-bitten cider, in the sky there was a brilliant, beautiful sun, in the wind was the tingling touch of three ice-chilled rivers. And in the big house facing Central Park, outside of which his prancing steed of brass and scarlet chugged and protested and trembled with impatience, was the most wonderful girl in all the world. It was true she was engaged to be married, and not to him. But she was not yet married. And to-day it would be his privilege to carry her through the State of New York and the State of Connecticut, and he would snatch glimpses of her profile rising from the rough fur collar, of her wind-blown hair, of the long, lovely lashes under the gray veil.

"Shall be together, breathe and ride, so, one day more am I deified," whispered the young man in the Scarlet Car; "who knows but the world may end to-night?'"

As he waited at the curb, other great touring-cars, of every speed and shape, in the mad race for the Boston Post Road, and the town of New Haven, swept up Fifth Avenue. Some rolled and puffed like tugboats in a heavy seaway, others glided by noiseless and proud as private yachts. But each flew the colors of blue or crimson.

Winthrop's car, because her brother had gone to one college, and he had played right end for the other, was draped impartially. And so every other car mocked or cheered it, and in one a bare-headed youth stood up, and shouted to his fellows: "Look! There's Billy Winthrop! Three times three for old Billy Winthrop!" And they lashed the air with flags and sent his name echoing over Central Park.

Winthrop grinned in embarrassment, and waved his hand. A bicycle cop, and Fred, the chauffeur, were equally impressed.

"Was they the Harvoids, sir?" asked Fred.

"They was," said Winthrop.

Her brother Sam came down the steps carrying sweaters and steamer-rugs. But he wore no holiday countenance.

"What do you think?" he demanded indignantly. "Ernest Peabody's inside making trouble. His sister has a Pullman on one of the special trains, and he wants Beatrice to go with her."

In spite of his furs, the young man in the car turned quite cold. "Not with us?" he gasped.

Miss Forbes appeared at the house door, followed by Ernest Peabody. He wore an expression of disturbed dignity; she one of distressed amusement. That she also wore her automobile coat caused the heart of Winthrop to leap hopefully.

"Winthrop," said Peabody, "I am in rather an embarrassing position. My sister, Mrs. Taylor Holbrooke"-- he spoke the name as though he were announcing it at the door of a drawing-room-- "desires Miss Forbes to go with her. She feels accidents are apt to occur with motor cars- and there are no other ladies in your party--and the crowds..."

Winthrop carefully avoided looking at Miss Forbes.

"I should be very sorry," he murmured.

"Ernest!" said Miss Forbes, "I explained it was impossible for me to go with your sister. We would be extremely rude to Mr. Winthrop. How do you wish us to sit?" she asked.

She mounted to the rear seat, and made room opposite her for Peabody.

"Do I understand, Beatrice," began Peabody in a tone that instantly made every one extremely uncomfortable, "that I am to tell my sister you are not coming?"

"Ernest!" begged Miss Forbes.

Winthrop bent hastily over the oil valves. He read the speedometer, which was, as usual, out of order, with fascinated interest.

"Ernest," pleaded Miss Forbes, "Mr. Winthrop and Sam planned this trip for us a long time ago- to give us a little pleasure..."

"Then," said Peabody in a hollow voice, "you have decided?"

"Ernest," cried Miss Forbes, "don't look at me as though you meant to hurl the curse of Rome. I have. Jump in. Please!"

"I will bid you good-by," said Peabody; "I have only just time to catch our train."

Miss Forbes rose and moved to the door of the car.

"I had better not go with any one," she said in a low voice.

"You will go with me," commanded her brother. "Come on, Ernest."

"Thank you, no," replied Peabody. "I have promised my sister."

"All right, then," exclaimed Sam briskly, "see you at the game. Section H. Don't forget. Let her out, Billy."

With a troubled countenance Winthrop bent forward and clasped the clutch.

"Better come, Peabody," he said.

"I thank you, no," repeated Peabody. "I must go with my sister."

As the car glided forward Brother Sam sighed heavily.

"My! but he's got a mean disposition," he said. "He has quite spoiled MY day."

He chuckled wickedly, but Winthrop pretended not to hear, and his sister maintained an expression of utter dejection.

But to maintain an expression of utter dejection is very difficult when the sun is shining, when you are flying at the rate of forty miles an hour, and when in the cars you pass foolish youths wave Yale flags at you, and take advantage of the day to cry: "Three cheers for the girl in the blue hat!"

Ernest Peabody

And to entirely remove the last trace of the gloom that Peabody had forced upon them, it was necessary only for a tire to burst. Of course for this effort, the tire chose the coldest and most fiercely windswept portion of the Pelham Road, where from the broad waters of the Sound pneumonia and the grip raced rampant, and where to the touch a steel wrench was not to be distinguished from a piece of ice. But before the wheels had ceased to complain, Winthrop and Fred were out of their fur coats, down on their knees, and jacking up the axle.

"On an expedition of this sort," said Brother Sam, "whatever happens, take it as a joke. Fortunately," he explained, "I don't understand fixing inner tubes, so I will get out and smoke. I have noticed that when a car breaks down, there is always one man who paces up and down the road and smokes. His hope is to fool passing cars into thinking that the people in his car stopped to admire the view."

Recognizing the annual football match as intended solely to replenish the town coffers, the thrifty townsfolk of Rye, with bicycles and red flags, were, as usual, and regardless of the speed at which it moved, levying tribute on every second car that entered their hospitable boundaries. But before the Scarlet Car reached Rye, small boys of the town, possessed of a sporting spirit, or of an inherited instinct for graft, were waiting to give a noisy notice of the ambush. And so, fore-warned, the Scarlet Car crawled up the main street of Rye as demurely as a baby-carriage, and then, having safely reached a point directly in front of the police station, with a loud and ostentatious report, blew up another tire.

"Well," said Sam crossly, "they can't arrest US for speeding."

"Whatever happens," said his sister, "take it as a joke."

Two miles outside of Stamford, Brother Sam burst into open mutiny.

"Every car in the United States has passed us," he declared.

"We won't get there, at this rate, till the end of the first half. Hit her up, can't you, Billy?"

"She seems to have an illness," said Winthrop unhappily. "I think I'd save time if I stopped now and fixed her."

Shamefacedly Fred and he hid themselves under the body of the car, and a sound of hammering and stentorian breathing followed. Of them all that was visible was four feet beating a tattoo on the road. Miss Forbes got out Winthrop's camera, and took a snap-shot of the scene.

"I will call it," she said, *The Idle Rich.*

Brother Sam gazed morosely in the direction of New Haven. They

Miss Forbes took a snapshot of the scene

had halted within fifty yards of the railroad tracks, and as each special train, loaded with happy enthusiasts, raced past them he groaned.

"The only one of us that showed any common sense was Ernest," he declared, "and you turned him down. I am going to take a trolley to Stamford, and the first train to New Haven."

"You are not," said his sister; "I will not desert Mr. Winthrop, and you cannot desert me."

Brother Sam sighed, and seated himself on a rock.

"Do you think, Billy," he asked, "you can get us to Cambridge in time for next year's game?"

The car limped into Stamford, and while it went into dry-dock at the garage, Brother Sam fled to the railroad station, where he learned that for the next two hours no train that recognized New Haven spoke to Stamford.

"That being so," said Winthrop, "while we are waiting for the car, we had better get a quick lunch now, and then push on."

"Push," exclaimed Brother Sam darkly, "is what we are likely to do."

After behaving with perfect propriety for half an hour, just outside of Bridgeport the Scarlet Car came to a slow and sullen stop, and once more the owner and the chauffeur hid their shame beneath it, and attacked its vitals. Twenty minutes later, while they still were at work, there approached from Bridgeport a young man in a buggy. When he saw the mass of college colors on the Scarlet Car, he pulled his horse down to a walk, and as he passed raised his hat. "At the end of the first half," he said, "the score was a tie."

"Don't mention it," said Brother Sam.

"Now," he cried, "we've got to turn back, and make for New York. If we start quick, we may get there ahead of the last car to leave New Haven."

"I am going to New Haven, and in this car," declared his sister. "I must go--to meet Ernest."

"If Ernest has as much sense as he showed this morning," returned her affectionate brother, "Ernest will go to his Pullman and stay there. As I told you, the only sure way to get anywhere is by railroad train."

When they passed through Bridgeport it was so late that the electric lights of Fairview Avenue were just beginning to sputter and glow in the twilight, and as they came along the shore road into New Haven, the first car out of New Haven in the race back to New York leaped at them with siren shrieks of warning, and dancing, dazzling eyes. It passed like a thing driven by the Furies; and before the Scarlet Car could swing back into what had been an empty road, in swift pursuit of the first came many more cars, with blinding searchlights, with a roar of throbbing, thrashing engines, flying pebbles, and whirling wheels. And behind these, stretching for a twisted mile, came hundreds of others; until the road was aflame with flashing Will-o'-the-wisps, dancing fireballs, and long, shifting shafts of light.

Miss Forbes sat in front, beside Winthrop, and it pleased her to imagine, as they bent forward, peering into the night, that together they were facing so many fiery dragons, speeding to give them battle, to grind them under their wheels. She felt the elation of great speed, of imminent danger. Her blood tingled with the air from the wind-swept harbor, with the rush of the great engines, as by a handbreadth they plunged past her. She knew they were driven by men and half-grown boys, joyous with victory, piqued by defeat, reckless by one touch too much of liquor, and that the young man at her side was driving, not only for himself, but for them.

Each fraction of a second a dazzling light blinded him, and he swerved to let the monster, with a hoarse, bellowing roar, pass by, and then again swept his car into the road. And each time for greater confidence she glanced up into his face.

Throughout the mishaps of the day he had been deeply concerned for her comfort, sorry for her disappointment, under Brother Sam's indignant ironies patient, and at all times gentle and considerate. Now, in the light from the onrushing cars, she noted his alert, laughing eyes, the broad shoulders bent across the wheel, the lips smiling with excitement and in the joy of controlling, with a turn of the wrist, a power equal to sixty galloping horses. She found in his face much comfort. And in the fact that for the moment her safety lay in his hands, a sense of pleasure. That this was her feeling puzzled and disturbed her, for to Ernest Peabody it seemed, in some way, disloyal. And yet there it was. Of a certainty, there was the secret pleasure in the thought that if they escaped unhurt from the trap in which they found themselves, it would be due to him. To herself she argued that if the chauffeur were driving, her feeling would be the same, that it was the nerve, the skill, and the coolness, not the man that moved her admiration. But in her heart she knew it would not be the same.

At West Haven Green Winthrop turned out of the track of the racing monsters into a quiet street leading to the railroad station, and with a half-sigh, half-laugh, leaned back comfortably.

"Those lights coming up suddenly make it hard to see," he said.

"Hard to breathe," snorted Sam; "since that first car missed us, I haven't drawn an honest breath. I held on so tight that I squeezed the hair out of the cushions."

When they reached the railroad station, and Sam had finally fought his way to the station master, that half-crazed official informed him he had missed the departure of Mrs. Taylor Holbrooke's car by just ten minutes.

Brother Sam reported this state of affairs to his companions.

"God knows we asked for the fish first," he said; "so now we've done our duty by Ernest, who has shamefully deserted us, and we can get something to eat, and go home at our leisure. As I have always told you, the only way to travel independently is in a touring-car."

At the New Haven House they bought three waiters, body and soul, and, in spite of the fact that in the very next room the team was breaking training, obtained an excellent but chaotic dinner; and by eight they were on their way back to the big city.

The night was grandly beautiful. The waters of the Sound flashed in the light of a cold, clear moon, which showed them, like pictures in silver print, the sleeping villages through which they passed, the ancient elms, the low-roofed cottages, the town hall facing the common. The post road was again empty, and the car moved as steadily as a watch.

"Just because it knows we don't care now when we get there," said Brother Sam, "you couldn't make it break down with an axe."

From the rear, where he sat with Fred, he announced he was going to sleep, and asked that he be not awakened until the car had crossed the State line between Connecticut and New York. Winthrop doubted if he knew the State line of New York.

"It is where the advertisements for Besse Baker's twenty-seven stores cease," said Sam drowsily, "and the billposters of Ethel Barrymore begin."

In the front of the car the two young people spoke only at intervals, but Winthrop had never been so widely alert, so keenly happy, never before so conscious of her presence.

And it seemed as they glided through the mysterious moonlit world of silent villages, shadowy woods, and wind-swept bays and inlets, from which, as the car rattled over the planks of the bridges, the wild duck rose in noisy circles, they alone were awake and living.

The silence had lasted so long that it was as eloquent as

words. The young man turned his eyes timorously, and sought those of the girl. What he felt was so strong in him that it seemed incredible she should be ignorant of it. His eyes searched the gray veil. In his voice there was both challenge and pleading.

"Shall be together," he quoted, "breathe and ride. So, one day more am I deified; who knows but the world may end tonight?"

The moonlight showed the girl's eyes shining through the veil, and regarding him steadily.

"If you don't stop this car quick," she said, "the world WILL end for all of us."

He shot a look ahead, and so suddenly threw on the brake that Sam and the chauffeur tumbled awake. Across the road stretched the great bulk of a touring-car, its lamps burning dully in the brilliance of the moon. Around it, for greater warmth, a half-dozen figures stamped upon the frozen ground, and beat themselves with their arms. Sam and the chauffeur vaulted into the road, and went toward them.

"It's what you say, and the way you say it," the girl explained. She seemed to be continuing an argument. "It makes it so very difficult for us to play together."

The young man clasped the wheel as though the force he were holding in check were much greater than sixty horsepower.

"You are not married yet, are you?" he demanded.

The girl moved her head.

"And when you are married, there will probably be an altar from which you will turn to walk back up the aisle?"

"Well?" said the girl.

"Well," he answered explosively, "until you turn away from that altar, I do not recognize the right of any man to keep me quiet, or your right either. Why should I be held by your engagement? I was not consulted about it. I did not give my consent, did I? I tell you, you are the only woman in the world I will ever marry, and if you think I am going to keep silent and watch some one else carry you off without making a fight for you, you don't know me."

"If you go on," said the girl, "it will mean that I shall not see you again."

"Then I will write letters to you."

"I will not read them," said the girl. The young man laughed defiantly.

"Oh, yes, you will read them!" He pounded his gauntleted fist on the rim of the wheel. "You mayn't answer them, but if I can write the way I feel, I will bet you'll read them."

His voice changed suddenly, and he began to plead. It was as though she were some masculine giant bullying a small boy.

"You are not fair to me," he protested. "I do not ask you to be kind, I ask you to be fair. I am fighting for what means more to me than anything in this world, and you won't even listen. Why should I recognize any other men! All I recognize is that I am the man who loves you, that I am the man at your feet. That is all I know, that I love you."

The girl moved as though with the cold, and turned her head from him.

"I love you," repeated the young man.

The girl breathed like one who has been swimming under water, but, when she spoke, her voice was calm and contained.

"Please!" she begged, "don't you see how unfair it is. I can't go away; I HAVE to listen."

The young man pulled himself upright, and pressed his lips together.

"I beg your pardon," he whispered.

There was for some time an unhappy silence, and then Winthrop added bitterly: "Methinks the punishment exceeds the offence."

"Do you think you make it easy for ME?" returned the girl.

She considered it most ungenerous of him to sit staring into the moonlight, looking so miserable that it made her heart ache to comfort him, and so extremely handsome that to do so was quite impossible. She would have liked to reach out her hand and lay it on his arm, and tell him she was sorry, but she could not. He should not have looked so unnecessarily handsome.

Sam came running toward them with five grizzly bears, who balanced themselves apparently with some slight effort upon their hind legs. The grizzly bears were properly presented as: "Tommy Todd, of my class, and some more like him. And," continued Sam, "I am going to quit you two and go with them. Tom's car broke down, but Fred fixed it, and both our cars can travel together. Sort of convoy," he explained.

His sister signaled eagerly, but with equal eagerness he retreated from her.

"Believe me," he assured her soothingly, "I am just as good a chaperon fifty yards behind you, and wide awake, as I am in the same car and fast asleep. And, besides, I want to hear about the game. And, what's more, two cars are much safer than one. Suppose you two break down in a lonely place? We'll be right behind you to pick you up. You will keep Winthrop's car in sight, won't you, Tommy?" he said.

The grizzly bear called Tommy, who had been examining the Scarlet Car, answered doubtfully that the only way he could keep it in sight was by tying a rope to it.

"That's all right, then," said Sam briskly, "Winthrop will go slow."

So the Scarlet Car shot forward with sometimes the second car so far in the rear that they could only faintly distinguish the horn begging them to wait, and again it would follow so close upon their wheels that they heard the five grizzly bears chanting beseechingly:

> Oh, bring this wagon home, John,
> It will not hold us a-all.

For some time there was silence in the Scarlet Car, and then Winthrop broke it by laughing.

"First, I lose Peabody," he explained, "then I lose Sam, and now, after I throw Fred overboard, I am going to drive you into Stamford, where they do not ask runaway couples for a license, and marry you."

The girl smiled comfortably. In that mood she was not afraid of him. She lifted her face, and stretched out her arms as though she were drinking in the moonlight.

"It has been such a good day," she said simply, "and I am really so very happy."

"I shall be equally frank," said Winthrop. "So am I."

For two hours they had been on the road, and were just entering Fairport. For some long time the voices of the pursuing grizzlies had been lost in the far distance.

"The road's up," said Miss Forbes.

She pointed ahead to two red lanterns.

"It was all right this morning," exclaimed Winthrop.

The car was pulled down to eight miles an hour, and, trembling and snorting at the indignity, nosed up to the red lanterns. They showed in a ruddy glow the legs of two men.

"You gotta stop!" commanded a voice.

"Why?" asked Winthrop.

The voice became embodied in the person of a tall man, with a long overcoat and a drooping mustache.

"Cause I tell you to!" snapped the tall man.

Winthrop threw a quick glance to the rear. In that direction for a mile the road lay straight away. He could see its entire length, and it was empty. In thinking of nothing but Miss Forbes, he had forgotten the chaperon. He was impressed with the fact that the immediate presence of a chaperon was desirable. Directly in front of the car, blocking its advance, were two barrels, with a two-inch plank sagging heavily between them. Beyond that the main street of Fairport lay steeped in slumber and moonlight.

"I am a selectman," said the one with the lantern. "You been exceedin' our speed limit."

The chauffeur gave a gasp that might have been construed to mean that the charge amazed and shocked him.

"That is not possible," Winthrop answered. "I have been going very slow--on purpose--to allow a disabled car to keep up with me."

The selectman looked down the road.

It ain't kep' up with you," he said pointedly.

"It has until the last few minutes."

"It's the last few minutes we're talking about," returned the man who had not spoken. He put his foot on the step of the car.

"What are you doing?" asked Winthrop.

"I am going to take you to Judge Allen's. I am chief of police. You are under arrest."

Before Winthrop rose moving pictures of Miss Forbes appearing in a dirty police station before an officious Dogberry, and, as he and his car were well known along the Post road, appearing the next morning in the New York papers. "William Winthrop," he saw the printed words, "son of Endicott Winthrop, was arrested here this evening, with a young woman who refused to give her name, but who was recognized as Miss Beatrice Forbes, whose engagement to Ernest Peabody, the Reform candidate on the Independent ticket..."

And, of course, Peabody would blame her.

"If I have exceeded your speed limit," he said politely, "I shall be delighted to pay the fine. How much is it?"

"Judge Allen'll tell you what the fine is," said the selectman gruffly. "And he may want bail."

"Bail?" demanded Winthrop. "Do you mean to tell me he will detain us here?"

"He will, if he wants to," answered the chief of police combatively.

For an instant Winthrop sat gazing gloomily ahead, overcome apparently by the enormity of his offence. He was calculating whether, if he rammed the two-inch plank, it would hit the car or Miss Forbes. He decided swiftly it would hit his new two-hundred-dollar lamps. As

"You been exceedin' our speed limit."

swiftly he decided the new lamps must go. But he had read of guardians of the public safety so regardless of private safety as to try to puncture runaway tires with pistol bullets. He had no intention of subjecting Miss Forbes to a fusillade.

So he whirled upon the chief of police:

"Take your hand off that gun!" he growled. "How dare you threaten me?"

Amazed, the chief of police dropped from the step and advanced indignantly.

"Me?" he demanded. "I ain't got a gun. What you mean by..."

With sudden intelligence, the chauffeur precipitated himself upon the scene.

"It's the other one," he shouted. He shook an accusing finger at the selectman. "He pointed it at the lady."

To Miss Forbes the realism of Fred's acting was too convincing. To learn that one is covered with a loaded revolver is disconcerting. Miss Forbes gave a startled squeak, and ducked her head.

Winthrop roared aloud at the selectman.

"How dare you frighten the lady!" he cried. "Take your hand off that gun."

"What you talkin' about?" shouted the selectman. "The idea of my havin' a gun! I haven't got a..."

"All right, Fred!" cried Winthrop. "Low bridge."

There was a crash of shattered glass and brass, of scattered barrel staves, the smell of escaping gas, and the Scarlet Car was flying drunkenly down the main street.

"What are they doing now, Fred?" called the owner.

Fred peered over the stern of the flying car.

"The constable's jumping around the road," he replied, "and the long one's leaning against a tree. No, he's climbing the tree. I can't make out WHAT he's doing."

"I know!" cried Miss Forbes; her voice vibrated with excitement. Defiance of the law had thrilled her with unsuspected satisfaction; her eyes were dancing. "There was a telephone fastened to the tree, a hand telephone. They are sending word to some one. They're trying to head us off." Winthrop brought the car to a quick halt.

"We're in a police trap!" he said. Fred leaned forward and whispered to his employer. His voice also vibrated with the joy of the chase.

"This'll be our THIRD arrest," he said. "That means..."

"I know what it means," snapped Winthrop. "Tell me how we can get out of here."

"We can't get out of here, sir, unless we go back. Going south, the bridge is the only way out."

"The bridge!" Winthrop struck the wheel savagely with his knuckles. "I forgot their confounded bridge!" He turned to Miss Forbes. "Fairport is a sort of island," he explained.

"But after we're across the bridge," urged the chauffeur, "we needn't keep to the post road no more. We can turn into Stone Ridge, and strike south to White Plains. Then..."

"We haven't crossed the bridge yet," growled Winthrop. His voice had none of the joy of the others; he was greatly perturbed. "Look back," he commanded, "and see if there is any sign of those boys."

He was now quite willing to share responsibility. But there was no sign of the Yale men, and, unattended, the Scarlet Car crept warily forward. Ahead of it, across the little reed-grown inlet, stretched their road of escape, a long wooden bridge, lying white in the moonlight.

"I don't see a soul," whispered Miss Forbes.

"Anybody at that draw?" asked Winthrop. Unconsciously his voice also had sunk to a whisper.

"No," returned Fred. "I think the man that tends the draw goes home at night; there is no light there."

"Well then," said Winthrop, with an anxious sigh, "we've got to make a dash for it."

The car shot forward, and, as it leaped lightly upon the bridge, there was a rapid rumble of creaking boards. Between it and the highway to New York lay only two hundred yards of track, straight and empty.

In his excitement the chauffeur rose from the rear seat. "They'll never catch us now," he muttered. "They'll never catch us!"

But even as he spoke there grated harshly the creak of rusty chains on a cogged wheel, the rattle of a brake. The black figure of a man with waving arms ran out upon the draw, and the draw gaped slowly open.

When the car halted there was between it and the broken edge of the bridge twenty feet of running water. At the same moment from behind it came a patter of feet, and Winthrop turned to see racing toward them some dozen young men of Fairport. They surrounded him with noisy, raucous, belligerent cries. They were, as they proudly informed him, members of the Fairport "Volunteer Fire Department." That they might purchase new uniforms, they had arranged a trap for the automobiles returning in illegal haste from New Haven. In fines they had

16

collected $300, and it was evident that already some of that money had been expended in bad whiskey. As many as could do so crowded into the car, others hung to the running boards and step, others ran beside it. They rejoiced over Winthrop's unsuccessful flight and capture with violent and humiliating laughter.

For the day, Judge Allen had made a temporary court in the clubroom of the fire department, which was over the engine house; and the proceedings were brief and decisive. The selectman told how Winthrop, after first breaking the speed law, had broken arrest and Judge Allen, refusing to fine him and let him go, held him and his companions for a hearing the following morning. He fixed the amount of bail at $500 each; failing to pay this, they would for the night be locked up in different parts of the engine house, which, it developed, contained on the ground floor the home of the fire engine, on the second floor the clubroom, on alternate nights, of the firemen, the local G.A.R., and the Knights of Pythias, and in its cellar the town jail.

Winthrop and the chauffeur the learned judge condemned to the cells in the basement. As a concession, he granted Miss Forbes the freedom of the entire clubroom to herself.

The objections raised by Winthrop to this arrangement were of a nature so violent, so vigorous, at one moment so specious and conciliatory, and the next so abusive, that his listeners were moved by awe, but not to pity.

In his indignation, Judge Allen rose to reply, and as, the better to hear him, the crowd pushed forward, Fred gave way before it, until he was left standing in sullen gloom upon its outer edge. In imitation of the real firemen of the great cities, the vamps of Fairport had cut a circular hole in the floor of their clubroom, and from the engine room below had reared a sliding pole of shining brass. When leaving their clubroom, it was always their pleasure to scorn the stairs and, like real firemen, slide down this pole. It had not escaped the notice of Fred, and since his entrance he had been gravitating toward it.

As the voice of the judge rose in violent objurgation, and all eyes were fixed upon him, the chauffeur crooked his leg tightly about the brass pole, and, like the devil in the pantomime, sank softly and swiftly through the floor.

The irate judge was shaking his finger in Winthrop's face.

"Don't you try to teach me no law," he shouted; "I know what I can do. Ef MY darter went gallivantin' around nights in one of them automobiles, it would serve her right to get locked up. Maybe this young woman will learn to stay at home nights with her folks. She ain't goin' to take no harm here. The constable sits up all night downstairs in the fire engine room, and that sofa's as good a place to sleep as the hotel. If you want me to let her go to the hotel, why don't you send to your folks and bail her out?"

"You know damn well why I don't," returned Winthrop. "I don't intend to give the newspapers and you and these other idiots the chance to annoy her further. This young lady's brother has been with us all day; he left us only by accident, and by forcing her to remain here alone you are acting outrageously. If you knew anything of decency, or law, you'd..."

"I know this much!" roared the justice triumphantly, pointing his spectacle-case at Miss Forbes. "I know her name ain't Lizzie Borden and yours ain't Charley Ross."

Winthrop crossed to where Miss Forbes stood in a corner. She still wore her veil, but through it, though her face was pale, she smiled at him.

His own distress was undisguised.

"I can never forgive myself," he said.

"Nonsense!" replied Miss Forbes briskly. "You were perfectly right. If we had sent for any one, it would have had to come out. Now, we'll pay the fine in the morning and get home, and no one will know anything of it excepting the family and Mr. Peabody, and they'll understand. But if I ever lay hands on my brother Sam!" she clasped her fingers together helplessly. "To think of his leaving you to spend the night in a cell..."

Winthrop interrupted her. "I will get one of these men to send his wife or sister over to stay with you," he said.

But Miss Forbes protested that she did not want a companion. The constable would protect her, she said, and she would sit up all night and read. She nodded at the periodicals on the club table.

"This is the only chance I may ever have," she said, "to read the *Police Gazette*!"

"You ready there?" called the constable.

"Good-night," said Winthrop.

Under the eyes of the grinning yokels, they shook hands.

"Good-night," said the girl.

"Where's your young man?" demanded the chief of police.

"My what?" inquired Winthrop.

"The young fellow that was with you when we held you up that first time."

The constable, or the chief of police as he called himself, on the principle that if there were only one policeman he must necessarily be the chief, glanced hastily over the heads of the crowd.

"Any of you holding that shoffer?" he called.

No one was holding the chauffeur.

The chauffeur had vanished.

The cell to which the constable led Winthrop was in a corner of the cellar in which formerly coal had been stored. This corner was now fenced off with boards, and a wooden door with chain and padlock.

High in the wall, on a level with the ground, was the opening, or window, through which the coal had been dumped. This window now was barricaded with iron bars. Winthrop tested the door by shaking it, and landed a heavy kick on one of the hinges. It gave slightly, and emitted a feeble groan.

"What you tryin' to do?" demanded the constable. "That's town property."

In the light of the constable's lantern, Winthrop surveyed his cell with extreme dissatisfaction.

"I call this a cheap cell," he said.

"It's good enough for a cheap sport," returned the constable. It was so overwhelming a retort that after the constable had turned the key in the padlock, and taken himself and his lantern to the floor above, Winthrop could hear him repeating it to the volunteer firemen. They received it with delighted howls.

For an hour, on the three empty boxes that formed his bed, Winthrop sat, with his chin on his fists, planning the nameless atrocities he would inflict upon the village of Fairport. Compared to his tortures, those of Neuremberg were merely reprimands. Also he considered the particular punishment he would mete out to Sam Forbes for his desertion of his sister, and to Fred. He could not understand Fred. It was not like the chauffeur to think only of himself. Nevertheless, for abandoning Miss Forbes in the hour of need, Fred must be discharged. He had, with some regret, determined upon this discipline, when from directly over his head the voice of Fred hailed him cautiously.

"Mr. Winthrop," the voice called, "are you there?"

To Winthrop the question seemed superfluous. He jumped to his feet, and peered up into the darkness.

"Where are YOU?" he demanded.

"At the window," came the answer. "We're in the back yard. Mr.

The moonlight was eclipsed by a head and shoulders

Sam wants to speak to you."

On Miss Forbes's account, Winthrop gave a gasp of relief. On his own, one of savage satisfaction.

"And I want to speak to HIM!" he whispered.

The moonlight, which had been faintly shining through the iron bars of the coal chute, was eclipsed by a head and shoulders. The comfortable voice of Sam Forbes greeted him in a playful whisper.

"Hullo, Billy! You down there?"

"Where the devil did you think I was?" Winthrop answered at white heat. "Let me tell you if I was not down here I'd be punching your head."

"That's all right, Billy," Sam answered soothingly. "But I'll save you just the same. It shall never be said of Sam Forbes he deserted a comrade..."

"Stop that! Do you know," Winthrop demanded fiercely, "that your sister is a prisoner upstairs?"

"I do," replied the unfeeling brother, "but she won't be long. All the low-comedy parts are out now arranging a rescue."

"Who are? Todd and those boys?" demanded Winthrop. "They mustn't think of it! They'll only make it worse. It is impossible to get your sister out of here with those drunken firemen in the building. You must wait till they've gone home. Do you hear me?"

"Pardon ME!" returned Sam stiffly, "but this is MY relief expedition. I have sent two of the boys to hold the bridge, like Horatius, and two to guard the motors, and the others are going to entice the firemen away from the engine house."

"Entice them? How?" demanded Winthrop. "They're drunk, and they won't leave here till morning."

Outside the engine house, suspended from a heavy cross-bar, was a steel rail borrowed from a railroad track, and bent into a hoop. When hit with a sledge-hammer it proclaimed to Fairport that the "consuming element" was at large.

At the moment Winthrop asked his question, over the village of Fairport and over the bay and marshes, and far out across the Sound, the great steel bar sent forth a shuddering boom of warning.

From the room above came a wild tumult of joyous yells.

"Fire!" shrieked the vamps, "fire!"

The two men crouching by the cellar window heard the rush of feet, the engine banging and bumping across the sidewalk, its brass bell clanking crazily, the happy vamps shouting hoarse, incoherent orders.

Through the window Sam lowered a bag of tools he had taken from Winthrop's car.

"Can you open the lock with any of these?" he asked.

"I can kick it open!" yelled Winthrop joyfully. "Get to your sister, quick!"

He threw his shoulder against the door, and the staples flying before him sent him sprawling in the coal-dust. When he reached the head of the stairs, Beatrice Forbes was descending from the clubroom, and in front of the door the two cars, with their lamps unlit and numbers hidden, were panting to be free.

And in the North, reaching to the sky, rose a roaring column of flame, shameless in the pale moonlight, dragging into naked day the sleeping village, the shingled houses, the clock-face in the church steeple.

"What the devil have you done?" gasped Winthrop.

Before he answered, Sam waited until the cars were rattling to safety across the bridge.

"We have been protecting the face of nature," he shouted. "The only way to get that gang out of the engine house was to set fire to something. Tommy wanted to burn up the railroad station, because he doesn't like the New York and New Haven, and Fred was for setting fire to Judge Allen's house, because he was rude to Beatrice. But we finally formed the Village Improvement Society, organized to burn all advertising signs. You know those that stood in the marshes, and hid the view from the trains, so that you could not see the Sound. We chopped them down and put them in a pile, and poured gasoline on them, and that fire is all that is left of the pickles, fly-screens, and pills."

It was midnight when the cars drew up at the door of the house of Forbes. Anxiously waiting in the library were Mrs. Forbes and Ernest Peabody.

"At last!" cried Mrs. Forbes, smiling her relief; "we thought maybe Sam and you had decided to spend the night in New Haven."

"No," said Miss Forbes, "there WAS some talk about spending the night at Fairport, but we pushed right on."

CHAPTER II
THE TRESPASSERS

With a long, nervous shudder, the Scarlet Car came to a stop, and the lamps bored a round hole in the night, leaving the rest of the encircling world in a chill and silent darkness.

The lamps showed a flickering picture of a country road between high banks covered with loose stones, and overhead, a fringe of pine boughs. It looked like a colored photograph thrown from a stereopticon in a darkened theater.

From the back of the car the voice of the owner said briskly: "We will now sing that beautiful ballad entitled *He Is Sleeping in the Yukon Vale Tonight*. What are you stopping for, Fred?" he asked.

The tone of the chauffeur suggested he was again upon the defensive.

"For water, sir," he mumbled.

Miss Forbes in the front seat laughed, and her brother in the rear seat, groaned in dismay.

"Oh, for water?" said the owner cordially. "I thought maybe it was for coal."

"There ought to be a house just about here"

Save a dignified silence, there was no answer to this, until there came a rolling of loose stones and the sound of a heavy body suddenly precipitated down the bank, and landing with a thump in the road.

"He didn't get the water," said the owner sadly.

"Are you hurt, Fred?" asked the girl.

The chauffeur limped in front of the lamps, appearing suddenly, like an actor stepping into the limelight.

"No, ma'am," he said. In the rays of the lamp, he unfolded a road map and scowled at it. He shook his head aggrievedly.

"There OUGHT to be a house just about here," he explained.

"There OUGHT to be a hotel and a garage, and a cold supper, just about here," said the girl cheerfully.

"That's the way with those houses," complained the owner. "They never stay where they're put. At night they go around and visit each other. Where do you think you are, Fred?"

"I think we're in that long woods, between Loon Lake and Stoughton on the Boston Pike," said the chauffeur, "and," he reiterated, "there OUGHT to be a house somewhere about here--where we get water."

"Well, get there, then, and get the water," commanded the owner.

"But I can't get there, sir, till I get the water," returned the chauffeur.

He shook out two collapsible buckets, and started down the shaft of light.

"I won't be more nor five minutes," he called.

"I'm going with him," said the girl, "I'm cold."

She stepped down from the front seat, and the owner with sudden alacrity vaulted the door and started after her.

"You coming?" he inquired of Ernest Peabody. But Ernest Peabody being soundly asleep made no reply.

Winthrop turned to Sam. "Are YOU coming?" he repeated.

The tone of the invitation seemed to suggest that a refusal would not necessarily lead to a quarrel.

"I am NOT!" said the brother. "You've kept Peabody and me twelve hours in the open air, and it's past two, and we're going to sleep. You can take it from me that we are going to spend the rest of this night here in this road."

He moved his cramped joints cautiously, and stretched his legs the full width of the car.

"If you can't get plain water," he called, "get club soda."

He buried his nose in the collar of his fur coat, and the odors of camphor and raccoon skins instantly assailed him, but he only yawned luxuriously and disappeared into the coat as a turtle draws into its shell. From the woods about him the smell of the pine needles pressed upon him like a drug, and before the footsteps of his companions were lost in the silence he was asleep. But his sleep was only a review of his waking hours. Still on either hand rose flying dust clouds and twirling leaves; still on either side raced gray stone walls, telegraph poles, hills rich in autumn colors; and before him a long white road, unending, interminable, stretching out finally into a darkness lit by flashing shop-windows, like open fireplaces, by street lamps, by swinging electric globes, by the blinding searchlights of hundreds of darting trolley cars with terrifying gongs, and then a cold white mist, and again on every side, darkness, except where the four great lamps blazed a path through stretches of ghostly woods.

As the two young men slumbered, the lamps spluttered and sizzled like bacon in a frying-pan, a stone rolled noisily down the bank, a white owl, both appalled and fascinated by the dazzling eyes of the monster blocking the road, hooted, and flapped itself away. But the men in the car only shivered slightly, deep in the sleep of utter weariness.

In silence the girl and Winthrop followed the chauffeur. They had passed out of the light of the lamps, and in the autumn mist the electric torch of the owner was as ineffective as a glow-worm. The mystery of the forest fell heavily upon them. From their feet the dead leaves sent up a clean, damp odor, and on either side and overhead the giant pine trees whispered and rustled in the night wind.

"Take my coat, too," said the young man. "You'll catch cold."

He spoke with authority and began to slip the loops from the big horn buttons. It was not the habit of the girl to consider her health. Nor did she permit the members of her family to show solicitude concerning it. But the anxiety of the young man, did not seem to offend her. She thanked him generously. "No; these coats are hard to walk in, and I want to walk," she exclaimed.

"I like to hear the leaves rustle when you kick them, don't you? When I was so high, I used to pretend it was wading in the surf."

The young man moved over to the gutter of the road where the leaves were deepest and kicked violently. "And the more noise you make," he said, "the more you frighten away the wild animals."

The girl shuddered in a most helpless and fascinating fashion.

"Don't!" she whispered. "I didn't mention it, but already I have seen several lions crouching behind the trees."

"Indeed?" said the young man. His tone was preoccupied. He had just kicked a rock, hidden by the leaves, and was standing on one leg.

"Do you mean you don't believe me?" asked the girl, "or is it that you are merely brave?"

"Merely brave!" exclaimed the young man. "Massachusetts is so far north for lions," he continued, "that I fancy what you saw was a grizzly bear. But I have my trusty electric torch with me, and if there is anything a bear cannot abide, it is to be pointed at by an electric torch."

"Let us pretend," cried the girl, "that we are the babes in the wood, and that we are lost."

"We don't have to pretend we're lost," said the man, "and as I remember it, the babes came to a sad end. Didn't they die, and didn't the birds bury them with leaves?"

"Sam and Mr. Peabody can be the birds," suggested the girl.

"Sam and Peabody hopping around with leaves in their teeth would look silly," objected the man, "I doubt if I could keep from laughing."

"Then," said the girl, "they can be the wicked robbers who came to kill the babes."

"Very well," said the man with suspicious alacrity, "let us be babes. If I have to die," he went on heartily, "I would rather die with you than live with any one else."

When he had spoken, although they were entirely alone in the world and quite near to each other, it was as though the girl could not hear him, even as though he had not spoken at all. After a silence, the girl said: "Perhaps it would be better for us to go back to the car."

"I won't do it again," begged the man.

"We will pretend," cried the girl, "that the car is a van and that we are gypsies, and we'll build a campfire, and I will tell your fortune."

"You are the only woman who can," muttered the young man.

The girl still stood in her tracks.

"You said--" she began.

"I know," interrupted the man, "but you won't let me talk seriously, so I joke. But some day--"

"Oh, look!" cried the girl. "There's Fred."

She ran from him down the road. The young man followed her slowly, his fists deep in the pockets of the great-coat, and kicking at the unoffending leaves.

The chauffeur was peering through a double iron gate hung between square brick posts. The lower hinge of one gate was broken, and that gate lurched forward leaving an opening. By the light of the electric torch they could see the beginning of a driveway, rough and weed-grown, lined with trees of great age and bulk, and an unkempt lawn, strewn with bushes, and beyond, in an open place bare of trees and illuminated faintly by the stars, the shadow of a house, black, silent, and forbidding.

"That's it," whispered the chauffeur. "I was here before. The well is over there."

The young man gave a gasp of astonishment.

"Why," he protested, "this is the Carey place! I should say we WERE lost. We must have left the road an hour ago. There's not another house within miles." But he made no movement to enter. "Of all places!" he muttered.

"Well, then," urged the girl briskly, "if there's no other house, let's tap Mr. Carey's well and get on."

"Do you know who he is?" asked the man.

The girl laughed. "You don't need a letter of introduction to take a bucket of water, do you?" she said.

"It's Philip Carey's house. He lives here." He spoke in a whisper, and insistently, as though the information must carry some special significance. But the girl showed no sign of enlightenment. "You remember the Carey boys?" he urged. "They left Harvard the year I entered. They HAD to leave. They were quite mad. All the Careys have been mad. The boys were queer even then, and awfully rich. Henry ran away with a girl from a shoe factory in Brockton and lives in Paris, and Philip was sent here."

"Sent here?" repeated the girl. Unconsciously her voice also had sunk to a whisper.

"He has a doctor and a nurse and keepers, and they live here all the year round. When Fred said there were people hereabouts, I thought we might strike them for something to eat, or even to put us up for the night, but, Philip Carey! I shouldn't fancy..."

"I should think not!" exclaimed the girl.

For, a minute the three stood silent, peering through the iron bars.

"And the worst of it is," went on the young man irritably, "he could give us such good things to eat."

"It doesn't look it," said the girl.

"I know," continued the man in the same eager whisper. "But--who was it was telling me? Some doctor I know who came down to see him. He said Carey does himself awfully well, has the house full of bully pictures, and the family plate, and wonderful collections- things he picked up in the East-- gold ornaments, and jewels, and jade."

"I shouldn't think," said the girl in the same hushed voice, "they would let him live so far from any neighbors with such things in the house. Suppose burglars..."

"Burglars! Burglars would never hear of this place. How could they? Even his friends think it's just a private madhouse."

The girl shivered and drew back from the gate.

Fred coughed apologetically.

"I'VE heard of it," he volunteered. "There was a piece in the Sunday Post. It said he eats his dinner in a diamond crown, and all the walls is gold, and two monkeys wait on table with gold..."

"Nonsense!" said the man sharply. "He eats like any one else and dresses like any one else. How far is the well from the house?"

"It's purty near," said the chauffeur.

"Pretty near the house, or pretty near here?"

"Just outside the kitchen; and it makes a creaky noise."

"You mean you don't want to go?"

Fred's answer was unintelligible.

"You wait here with Miss Forbes," said the young man. "And I'll get the water."

"Yes, sir!" said Fred, quite distinctly.

"No, sir!" said Miss Forbes, with equal distinctness. "I'm not going to be left here alone--with all these trees. I'm going with you."

"There may be a dog," suggested the young man, "or, I was thinking if they heard me prowling about, they might take a shot- just for luck. Why don't you go back to the car with Fred?"

"Down that long road in the dark?" exclaimed the girl. "Do you think I have no imagination?"

The man in front, the girl close on his heels, and the boy with the buckets following, crawled through the broken gate, and moved cautiously up the gravel driveway. Within fifty feet of the house the courage of the chauffeur returned.

"You wait here," he whispered, "and if I wake 'em up, you shout to 'em that it's all right, that it's only me."

"Your idea being," said the young man, "that they will then fire at me. Clever lad. Run along."

There was a rustling of the dead weeds, and instantly the chauffeur was swallowed in the encompassing shadows.

Miss Forbes leaned toward the young man. "Do you see a light in that lower story?" she whispered.

"No," said the man. "Where?"

After a pause the girl answered: "I can't see it now, either. Maybe I didn't see it. It was very faint- just a glow- it might have been phosphorescence."

"It might," said the man. He gave a shrug of distaste. "The whole place is certainly old enough and decayed enough."

For a brief space they stood quite still, and at once, accentuated by their own silence, the noises of the night grew in number and distinctness. A slight wind had risen and the boughs of the pines rocked restlessly, making mournful complaint; and at their feet the needles dropping in a gentle desultory shower had the sound of rain in springtime. From every side they were startled by noises they could not place. Strange movements and rustlings caused them to peer sharply into the shadows; footsteps, that seemed to approach, and, then, having marked them, skulk away; branches of bushes that suddenly swept together, as though closing behind some one in stealthy retreat. Although they knew that in the deserted garden they were alone, they felt that from the shadows they were being spied upon, that the darkness of the place was peopled by malign presences.

The young man drew a cigar from his case and put it unlit between his teeth.

"Cheerful, isn't it?" he growled. "These dead leaves make it damp as a tomb. If I've seen one ghost, I've seen a dozen. I believe we're standing in the Carey family's graveyard."

"I thought you were brave," said the girl.

"I am," returned the young man, "very brave. But if you had the most wonderful girl on earth to take care of in the grounds of a madhouse at two in the morning, you'd be scared too."

He was abruptly surprised by Miss Forbes laying her hand firmly upon his shoulder, and turning him in the direction of the house. Her face was so near his that he felt the uneven fluttering of her breath upon his cheek.

"There is a man," she said, "standing behind that tree."

By the faint light of the stars he saw, in black silhouette, a shoulder and head projecting from beyond the trunk of a huge oak, and then quickly withdrawn. The owner of the head and shoulder was on the side of the tree nearest to themselves, his back turned to them, and so deeply was his attention engaged that he was unconscious of their presence.

"He is watching the house," said the girl. "Why is he doing that?"

In the two circles of light the men surveyed each other

"I think it's Fred," whispered the man. "He's afraid to go for the water. That's as far as he's gone." He was about to move forward when from the oak tree there came a low whistle.

The girl and the man stood silent and motionless. But they knew it was useless; that they had been overheard. A voice spoke cautiously.

"That you?" it asked.

With the idea only of gaining time, the young man responded promptly and truthfully. "Yes," he whispered.

"Keep to the right of the house," commanded the voice.

The young man seized Miss Forbes by the wrist and moving to the right drew her quickly with him. He did not stop until they had turned the corner of the building, and were once more hidden by the darkness.

"The plot thickens," he said. "I take it that that fellow is a keeper, or watchman. He spoke as though it were natural there should be another man in the grounds, so there's probably two of them, either to keep Carey in, or to keep trespassers out. Now, I think I'll go back and tell him that Jack and Jill went up the hill to fetch a pail of water, and that all they want is to be allowed to get the water, and go."

"Why should a watchman hide behind a tree?" asked the girl. "And why..."

She ceased abruptly with a sharp cry of fright. "What's that?" she whispered.

"What's what?" asked the young man startled. "What did you hear?"

"Over there," stammered the girl. "Something-- that--groaned."

"Pretty soon this will get on my nerves," said the man. He ripped open his greatcoat and reached under it. "I've been stoned twice, when there were women in the car," he said, apologetically, "and so now at night I carry a gun." He shifted the darkened torch to his left hand, and, moving a few yards, halted to listen. The girl, reluctant to be left alone, followed slowly. As he stood immovable there came from the leaves just beyond him the sound of a feeble struggle, and a strangled groan. The man bent forward and flashed the torch. He saw stretched rigid on the ground a huge wolf-hound. Its legs were twisted horribly, the lips drawn away from the teeth, the eyes glazed in an agony of pain. The man snapped off the light. "Keep back!" he whispered to the girl. He took her by the arm and ran with her toward the gate.

"Who was it?" she begged.

"It was a dog," he answered. "I think..."

He did not tell her what he thought.

"I've got to find out what the devil has happened to Fred!" he said. "You go back to the car. Send your brother here on the run. Tell him there's going to be a rough-house. You're not afraid to go?"

"No," said the girl.

A shadow blacker than the night rose suddenly before them, and a voice asked sternly but quietly: "What are you doing here?"

The young man lifted his arm clear of the girl, and shoved her quickly from him. In his hand she felt the pressure of the revolver.

"Well," he replied truculently, "and what are you doing here?"

"I am the night watchman," answered the voice. "Who are you?"

It struck Miss Forbes if the watchman knew that one of the trespassers was a woman he would be at once reassured, and she broke in quickly:

"We have lost our way," she said pleasantly. "We came here..."

She found herself staring blindly down a shaft of light. For an instant the torch held her, and then from her swept over the young man.

"Drop that gun!" cried the voice. It was no longer the same voice; it was now savage and snarling. For answer the young man pressed the torch in his left hand, and, held in the two circles of light, the men surveyed each other. The newcomer was one of unusual bulk and height. The collar of his overcoat hid his mouth, and his derby hat was drawn down over his forehead, but what they saw showed an intelligent, strong face, although for the moment it wore a menacing scowl. The young man dropped his revolver into his pocket.

"My automobile ran dry," he said; "we came in here to get some water. My chauffeur is back there somewhere with a couple of buckets. This is Mr. Carey's place, isn't it?"

"Take that light out of my eyes!" said the watchman.

"Take your light out of my eyes," returned the young man. "You can see we're not-- we don't mean any harm."

The two lights disappeared simultaneously, and then each, as though worked by the same hand, sprang forth again.

"What did you think I was going to do?" the young man asked. He laughed and switched off his torch.

But the one the watchman held in his hand still moved from the face of the girl to that of the young man.

"How'd you know this was the Carey house?" he demanded. "Do you know Mr. Carey?"

"No, but I know this is his house." For a moment from behind his mask of light the watchman surveyed them in silence. Then he spoke quickly: "I'll take you to him," he said, "if he thinks it's all right, it's all right."

The girl gave a protesting cry. The young man burst forth indignantly: "You will NOT!" he cried. "Don't be an idiot! You talk like a Tenderloin cop. Do we look like second-story workers?"

"I found you prowling around Mr. Carey's grounds at two in the morning," said the watchman sharply, "with a gun in your hand. My job is to protect this place, and I am going to take you both to Mr. Carey."

Until this moment the young man could see nothing save the shaft of light and the tiny glowing bulb at its base; now into the light there protruded a black revolver.

"Keep your hands up, and walk ahead of me to the house," commanded the watchman. "The woman will go in front."

The young man did not move. Under his breath he muttered impotently, and bit at his lower lip. "See here," he said, "I'll go with you, but you shan't take this lady in front of that madman. Let her go to her car. It's only a hundred yards from here; you know perfectly well she..."

"I know where your car is, all right," said the watchman steadily, "and I'm not going to let you get away in it till Mr. Carey's seen you." The revolver motioned forward. Miss Forbes stepped in front of it and appealed eagerly to the young man.

"Do what he says," she urged. "It's only his duty. Please! Indeed, I don't mind." She turned to the watchman. "Which way do you want us to go?" she asked.

"Keep in the light," he ordered.

The light showed the broad steps leading to the front entrance of the house, and in its shaft they climbed them, pushed open the unlocked door, and stood in a small hallway. It led into a greater hall beyond. By the electric lights still burning they noted that the interior of the house was as rich and well cared for as the outside was miserable. With a gesture for silence the watchman motioned them into a small room on the right of the hallway. It had the look of an office, and was apparently the place in which were conducted the affairs of the estate. In an open grate was a dying fire; in front of it a flat desk covered with papers and japanned tin boxes.

"You stay here till I fetch Mr. Carey, and the servants," commanded the watchman. "Don't try to get out, and," he added menacingly, "don't make no noise." With his revolver he pointed at the two windows. They were heavily barred. "Those bars keep Mr. Carey in," he

The girl shrinking against the wall

said, "and I guess they can keep you in, too. The other watchman," he added, "will be just outside this door." But still he hesitated, glowering with suspicion; unwilling to trust them alone. His face lit with an ugly smile. "Mr. Carey's very bad to-night," he said; "he won't keep his bed and he's wandering about the house. If he found you by yourselves, he might..."

The young man, who had been staring at the fire, swung sharply on his heel.

"Get-to-hell-out-of-here!" he said. The watchman stepped into the hall and was cautiously closing the door when a man sprang lightly up the front steps. Through the inch crack left by the open door the tres- passers heard the newcomer's eager greeting.

"I can't get him right!" he panted. "He's snoring like a hog."

The watchman exclaimed savagely: "He's fooling you." He gasped. "I didn't mor' nor slap him. Did you throw water on him?"

"I drowned him!" returned the other. "He never winked. I tell You we gotta walk, and damn quick!"

"Walk!" The watchman cursed him foully. "How far could we walk? I'LL bring him to," he swore. "He's scared of us, and he's sham- ming." He gave a sudden start of alarm. "That's it, he's shamming. You fool! You shouldn't have left him."

There was the swift patter of retreating footsteps, and then a sudden halt, and they heard the watchman command: "Go back, and keep the other two till I come."

The next instant from the outside the door was softly closed upon them.

It had no more than shut when to the surprise of Miss Forbes the young man, with a delighted and vindictive chuckle, sprang to the desk and began to drum upon it with his fingers. It were as though he were practicing upon a typewriter.

"He missed THESE," he muttered jubilantly. The girl leaned for- ward. Beneath his fingers she saw, flush with the table, a roll of little ivory buttons. She read the words "Stables, Servants' Hall." She raised a pair of very beautiful and very bewildered eyes.

"But if he wanted the servants, why didn't the watchman do that?" she asked.

"Because he isn't a watchman," answered the young man. "Because he's robbing this house."

He took the revolver from his encumbering greatcoat, slipped it in his pocket, and threw the coat from him. He motioned the girl into a corner. "Keep out of the line of the door," he ordered.

"I don't understand," begged the girl.

"They came in a car," whispered the young man. "It's broken down, and they can't get away. When the big fellow stopped us and I flashed my torch, I saw their car behind him in the road with the front off and the lights out. He'd seen the lamps of our car, and now they want it to escape in. That's why he brought us here- to keep us away from our car."

"And Fred!" gasped the girl. "Fred's hurt!"

"I guess Fred stumbled into the big fellow," assented the young man, "and the big fellow put him out; then he saw Fred was a chauffeur, and now they are trying to bring him to, so that he can run the car for them. You needn't worry about Fred. He's been in four smash-ups."

The young man bent forward to listen, but from no part of the great house came any sign. He exclaimed angrily. "They must be drugged," he growled. He ran to the desk and made vicious jabs at the ivory buttons. "Suppose they're out of order!" he whispered.

There was the sound of leaping feet. The young man laughed nervously.

"No, it's all right," he cried. "They're coming!"

The door flung open and the big burglar and a small, rat-like figure of a man burst upon them; the big one pointing a revolver.

"Come with me to your car!" he commanded. "You've got to take us to Boston. Quick, or I'll blow your face off."

Although the young man glared bravely at the steel barrel and the lifted trigger, poised a few inches from his eyes, his body, as though weak with fright, shifted slightly and his feet made a shuffling noise upon the floor. When the weight of his body was balanced on the ball of his right foot, the shuffling ceased. Had the burglar lowered his eyes, the maneuver to him would have been significant, but his eyes were following the barrel of the revolver.

In the mind of the young man the one thought uppermost was that he must gain time, but, with a revolver in his face, he found his desire to gain time swiftly diminishing. Still, when he spoke, it was with deliberation.

"My chauffeur..." he began slowly.

The burglar snapped at him like a dog. "To hell with your chauffeur!" he cried. "Your chauffeur has run away. You'll drive that car yourself, or I'll leave you here with the top of your head off."

The face of the young man suddenly flashed with pleasure. His eyes,

"You've broken the bone," he said

looking past the burglar to the door, lit with relief.

"There's the chauffeur now!" he cried.

The big burglar for one instant glanced over his right shoulder.

For months at a time, on Soldiers Field, the young man had thrown himself at human targets, that ran and dodged and evaded him, and the hulking burglar, motionless before him, was easily his victim. He leaped at him, his left arm swinging like a scythe, and, with the impact of a club, the blow caught the burglar in the throat.

The pistol went off impotently; the burglar with a choking cough sank in a heap on the floor. The young man tramped over him and upon him, and beat the second burglar with savage, whirlwind blows. The second burglar, shrieking with pain, turned to fly, and a fist, that fell upon him where his bump of honesty should have been, drove his head against the lintel of the door. At the same instant from the belfry on the roof there rang out on the night the sudden tumult of a bell; a bell that told as plainly as though it clamored with a human tongue, that the hand that rang it was driven with fear; fear of fire, fear of thieves, fear of a mad-man with a knife in his hand running amuck; perhaps at that moment creeping up the belfry stairs.

From all over the house there was the rush of feet and men's voices, and from the garden the light of dancing lanterns. And while the smoke of the revolver still hung motionless, the open door was crowded with half-clad figures. At their head were two young men. One who had drawn over his night clothes a serge suit, and who, in even that garb, carried an air of authority; and one, tall, stooping, weak of face and light-haired, with eyes that blinked and trembled behind great spectacles and who, for comfort, hugged about him a gorgeous kimono. For an instant the newcomers stared stupidly through the smoke at the bodies on the floor breathing stertorously, at the young man with the lust of battle still in his face, at the girl shrinking against the wall. It was the young man in the serge suit who was the first to move.

"Who are you?" he demanded.

"These are burglars," said the owner of the car. "We happened to be passing in my automobile, and..."

The young man was no longer listening. With an alert, professional manner he had stooped over the big burglar. With his thumb he pushed back the man's eyelids, and ran his fingers over his throat and chin. He felt carefully of the point of the chin, and glanced up.

"You've broken the bone," he said.

"I just swung on him," said the young man. He turned his eyes, and suggested the presence of the girl.

At the same moment the man in the kimono cried nervously: "Ladies present, ladies present. Go put your clothes on, everybody; put your clothes on."

For orders the men in the doorway looked to the young man with the stern face. He scowled at the figure in the kimono.

"You will please go to your room, sir," he said. He stood up, and bowed to Miss Forbes. "I beg your pardon," he asked, "you must want to get out of this. Will you please go into the library?"

He turned to the robust youths in the door, and pointed at the second burglar. "Move him out of the way," he ordered.

The man in the kimono smirked and bowed. "Allow me," he said; "allow me to show you to the library. This is no place for ladies."

The young man with the stern face frowned impatiently. "You will please return to your room, sir," he repeated.

With an attempt at dignity the figure in the kimono gathered the silk robe closer about him. "Certainly," he said. "If you think you can get on without me, I will retire," and lifting his bare feet mincingly, he tiptoed away. Miss Forbes looked after him with an expression of relief, of repulsion, of great pity.

The owner of the car glanced at the young man with the stern face, and raised his eyebrows interrogatively. The young man had taken the revolver from the limp fingers of the burglar and was holding it in his hand. Winthrop gave what was half a laugh and half a sigh of compassion.

"So, that's Carey?" he said.

There was a sudden silence. The young man with the stern face made no answer. His head was bent over the revolver. He broke it open, and spilled the cartridges into his palm. Still he made no answer. When he raised his head, his eyes were no longer stern, but wistful, and filled with an inexpressible loneliness.

"No, I am Carey," he said.

The one who had blundered stood helpless, tongue-tied, with no presence of mind beyond knowing that to explain would offend further. The other seemed to feel for him more than for himself. In a voice low and peculiarly appealing, he continued hurriedly.

"He is my doctor," he said. "He is a young man, and he has not had many advantages-- his manner is not-- I find we do not get on together. I have asked them to send me some one else." He stopped suddenly, and stood unhappily silent. The knowledge that the strangers were acquainted with his story seemed to rob him of his earlier confidence. He made an uncertain movement as though to relieve them of his presence.

Miss Forbes stepped toward him eagerly. "You told me I might wait in the library," she said. "Will you take me there?"

For a moment the man did not move, but stood looking at the young and beautiful girl, who, with a smile, hid the compassion in her eyes.

"Will you go?" he asked wistfully.

"Why not?" said the girl.

The young man laughed with pleasure.

"I am unpardonable," he said. "I live so much alone-- that I forget." Like one who, issuing from a close room, encounters the morning air, he drew a deep, happy breath. "It has been three years since a woman has been in this house," he said simply. "And I have not even thanked you," he went on, "nor asked you if you are cold," he cried remorsefully, "or hungry. How nice it would be if you would say you are hungry."

The girl walked beside him, laughing lightly, and, as they disappeared into the greater hall beyond, Winthrop heard her cry: "You never robbed your own ice-chest? How have you kept from starving? Show me it, and we'll rob it together."

The voice of their host rang through the empty house with a laugh like that of an eager, happy child.

"Heavens!" said the owner of the car, "isn't she wonderful!" But neither the prostrate burglars, nor the servants, intent on strapping their wrists together, gave him any answer.

As they were finishing the supper filched from the ice-chest, Fred was brought before them from the kitchen. The blow the burglar had given him was covered with a piece of cold beef-steak, and the water thrown on him to revive him was thawing from his leather breeches. Mr. Carey expressed his gratitude, and rewarded him beyond the avaricious dreams even of a chauffeur.

As the three trespassers left the house, accompanied by many pails of water, the girl turned to the lonely figure in the doorway and waved her hand.

"May we come again?" she called.

But young Mr. Carey did not trust his voice to answer. Standing erect, with folded arms, in dark silhouette in the light of the hall, he bowed his head.

Deaf to alarm bells, to pistol shots, to cries for help, they found her brother and Ernest Peabody sleeping soundly.

"Sam is a charming chaperon," said the owner of the car.

With the girl beside him, with Fred crouched, shivering, on the step, he threw in the clutch; the servants from the house waved the emptied buckets in salute, and the great car sprang forward into the awakening day toward the golden dome over the Boston Common. In the rear seat Peabody shivered and yawned, and then sat erect.

"Did you get the water?" he demanded, anxiously.

There was a grim silence.

"Yes," said the owner of the car patiently. "You needn't worry any longer. We got the water."

CHAPTER III
THE KIDNAPPERS

During the last two weeks of the "whirlwind" campaign, automobiles had carried the rival candidates to every election district in Greater New York.

During these two weeks, at the disposal of Ernest Peabody-- on the Reform Ticket, "the people's choice for Lieutenant-Governor--" Winthrop had placed his Scarlet Car, and, as its chauffeur, himself.

Not that Winthrop greatly cared for Reform, or Ernest Peabody. The "whirlwind" part of the campaign was what attracted him; the crowds, the bands, the fireworks, the rush by night from hall to hall, from Fordham to Tompkinsville. And, while inside the different Lyceums, Peabody lashed the Tammany Tiger, outside in his car, Winthrop was making friends with Tammany policemen, and his natural enemies, the bicycle cops. To Winthrop, the day in which he did not increase his acquaintance with the traffic squad, was a day lost.

But the real reason for his efforts in the cause of Reform, was one he could not declare. And it was a reason that was guessed perhaps by only one person. On some nights Beatrice Forbes and her brother Sam accompanied Peabody. And while Peabody sat in the rear of the car, mumbling the speech he would next deliver, Winthrop was given the chance to talk with her. These chances were growing cruelly few. In one month after election day Miss Forbes and Peabody would be man and wife. Once before the day of their marriage had been fixed, but, when the Reform Party offered Peabody a high place on its ticket, he asked, in order that he might bear his part in the cause of reform, that the wedding be postponed. To the postponement Miss Forbes made no objection. To one less self-centered than Peabody, it might have appeared that she almost too readily consented.

"I knew I could count upon your seeing my duty as I saw it," said Peabody much pleased, "it always will be a satisfaction to both of us to remember you never stood between me and my work for reform."

"What do you think my brother-in-law-to-be has done now?" demanded Sam of Winthrop, as the Scarlet Car swept into Jerome Avenue. "He's postponed his marriage with Trix just because he has a chance to be Lieutenant-Governor. What is a Lieutenant-Governor anyway, do you know? I don't like to ask Peabody."

"It is not his own election he's working for," said Winthrop. He was conscious of an effort to assume a point of view both noble and magnanimous. "He probably feels the 'cause' calls him. But, good Heavens!"

"Look out!" shrieked Sam, "where you going?"

Winthrop swung the car back into the avenue.

"To think," he cried, "that a man who could marry--a girl, and then would ask her to wait two months. Or, two days! Two months lost out of his life, and she might die; he might lose her, she might change her mind. Any number of men can be Lieutenant-Governors; only one man can be..."

He broke off suddenly, coughed and fixed his eyes miserably on the road. After a brief pause, Brother Sam covertly looked at him. Could it be that "Billie" Winthrop, the man liked of all men, should love his sister, and that she should prefer Ernest Peabody? He was deeply, loyally indignant. He determined to demand of his sister an immediate and abject apology.

At eight o'clock on the morning of election day, Peabody, in the Scarlet Car, was on his way to vote. He lived at Riverside Drive, and the polling-booth was only a few blocks distant. During the rest of the day he intended to use the car to visit other election districts, and to keep him in touch with the Reformers at the Gilsey House. Winthrop was acting as his chauffeur, and in the rear seat was Miss Forbes. Peabody had asked her to accompany him to the polling-booth, because he thought women who believed in reform should show their interest in it in public, before all men. Miss Forbes disagreed with him, chiefly because whenever she sat in a box at any of the public meetings the artists from the newspapers, instead of immortalizing the candidate, made pictures of her and her hat. After she had seen her future lord and master cast his vote for reform and himself, she was to depart by train to Tarrytown. The Forbes's country place was there, and for election day her brother Sam had invited out some of his friends to play tennis.

As the car darted and dodged up Eighth Avenue, a man who had been hidden by the stairs to the Elevated, stepped in front of it. It caught him, and hurled him, like a mail-bag tossed from a train, against one of the pillars that support the overhead tracks. Winthrop gave a cry and fell upon the brakes. The cry was as full of pain as though he himself had been mangled. Miss Forbes saw only the man appear, and then disappear, but, Winthrop's shout of warning, and the wrench as the brakes locked, told her what had happened. She shut her eyes, and for an instant covered them with her hands. On the front seat Peabody clutched helplessly at the cushions. In horror his eyes were fastened on the motionless mass jammed against the pillar. Winthrop scrambled over him, and ran to where the man lay. So, apparently, did every other inhabitant of Eighth Avenue; but Winthrop was the first to reach him and kneeling in the car tracks, he tried to place the head and shoulders of the body against the iron pillar. He had seen very few dead men; and to him, this weight in his arms, this bundle of limp flesh and muddy clothes, and the purple-bloated face with blood trickling down it, looked like a dead man.

Once or twice when in his car, death had reached for Winthrop, and only by the scantiest grace had he escaped. Then the nearness of it had only sobered him. Now that he believed he had brought it to a fellow man, even though he knew he was in no degree to blame, the thought sickened and shocked him. His brain trembled with remorse and horror.

But voices assailing him on every side brought him to the necessity of the moment. Men were pressing close upon him, jostling, abusing him, shaking fists in his face. Another crowd of men, as though fearing the car would escape of its own volition, were clinging to the steps and running boards.

Winthrop saw Miss Forbes standing above them, talking eagerly to Peabody, and pointing at him. He heard children's shrill voices calling to new arrivals that an automobile had killed a man; that it had killed him on purpose. On the outer edge of the crowd men shouted: "Ah, soak him," "Kill him," "Lynch him."

A soiled giant without a collar stooped over the purple, blood-stained face, and then leaped upright, and shouted: "It's Jerry Gaylor, he's

He tried to place the head and shoulders of the body against the iron pillar

killed old man Gaylor." The response was instant. Every one seemed to know Jerry Gaylor.

Winthrop took the soiled person by the arm. "You help me lift him into my car," he ordered. "Take him by the shoulders. We must get him to a hospital."

"To a hospital? To the Morgue!" roared the man. "And the police station for yours. You don't do no get-away."

Winthrop answered him by turning to the crowd. "If this man has any friends here, they'll please help me put him in my car, and we'll take him to Roosevelt Hospital."

The soiled person shoved a fist and a bad cigar under Winthrop's nose.

"Has he got any friends?" he mocked. "Sure, he's got friends, and they'll fix you, all right."

"Sure!" echoed the crowd.

The man was encouraged. "Don't you go away thinking you can come up here with your buzz wagon and murder better men nor you'll ever be and..."

"Oh, shut up!" said Winthrop.

He turned his back on the soiled man, and again appealed to the crowd.

"Don't stand there doing nothing," he commanded. "Do you want this man to die? Some of you ring for an ambulance and get a police-man, or tell me where is the nearest drug store."

No one moved, but every one shouted to every one else to do as Winthrop suggested.

Winthrop felt something pulling at his sleeve, and turning, found Peabody at his shoulder peering fearfully at the figure in the street. He had drawn his cap over his eyes and hidden the lower part of his face in the high collar of his motor coat. "I can't do anything, can I?" he asked.

"I'm afraid not," whispered Winthrop. "Go back to the car and don't leave Beatrice. I'll attend to this."

"That's what I thought," whispered Peabody eagerly. "I thought she and I had better keep out of it."

"Right!" exclaimed Winthrop. "Go back and get Beatrice away."

Peabody looked his relief, but still hesitated.

"I can't do anything, as you say," he stammered, "and it's sure to get in the 'extras,' and they'll be out in time to lose us thousands of votes, and though no one is to blame, they're sure to blame me. I don't care about myself," he added eagerly, "but the very morning of election--

half the city has not voted yet-- the Ticket..."

"Damn the Ticket!" exclaimed Winthrop. "The man's dead!"

Peabody, burying his face still deeper in his collar, backed into the crowd. In the present and past campaigns, from carts and automobiles he had made many speeches in Harlem, and on the West Side, lithographs of his stern, resolute features hung in every delicatessen shop, and that he might be recognized, was extremely likely.

He whispered to Miss Forbes what he had said, and what Winthrop had said.

"But you DON'T mean to leave him," remarked Miss Forbes.

"I must," returned Peabody. "I can do nothing for the man, and you know how Tammany will use this- They'll have it on the street by ten. They'll say I was driving recklessly; without regard for human life. And, besides, they're waiting for me at headquarters. Please hurry. I am late now."

Miss Forbes gave an exclamation of surprise. "Why, I'm not going," she said.

"You must go! I must go. You can't remain here alone." Peabody spoke in the quick, assured tone that at the first had convinced Miss Forbes his was a most masterful manner.

"Winthrop, too," he added, "wants you to go away."

Miss Forbes made no reply. But she looked at Peabody inquiringly, steadily, as though she were puzzled as to his identity, as though he had just been introduced to her. It made him uncomfortable.

"Are you coming?" he asked.

Her answer was a question.

"Are you going?"

"I am!" returned Peabody. He added sharply: "I must."

"Good-by," said Miss Forbes.

As he ran up the steps to the station of the elevated, it seemed to Peabody that the tone of her "good-by" had been most unpleasant. It was severe, disapproving. It had a final, fateful sound. He was conscious of a feeling of self-dissatisfaction. In not seeing the political importance of his not being mixed up with this accident, Winthrop had been peculiarly obtuse, and Beatrice, unsympathetic. Until he had cast his vote for Reform, he felt distinctly ill-used.

For a moment Beatrice Forbes sat in the car motionless, staring unseeingly at the iron steps by which Peabody had disappeared. For a few moments her brows were tightly drawn. Then, having apparently quickly arrived at some conclusion, she opened the door of the car and pushed into the crowd.

Winthrop received her most rudely. "You mustn't come here!" he cried.

"I thought," she stammered, "you might want some one?"

"I told-- " began Winthrop, and then stopped, and added-- "to take you away. Where is he?"

Miss Forbes flushed slightly. "He's gone," she said.

In trying not to look at Winthrop, she saw the fallen figure, motionless against the pillar, and with an exclamation, bent fearfully toward it.

"Can I do anything?" she asked.

The crowd gave way for her, and with curious pleased faces, closed in again eagerly. She afforded them a new interest.

A young man in the uniform of an ambulance surgeon was kneeling beside the mud-stained figure, and a police officer was standing over both. The ambulance surgeon touched lightly the matted hair from which the blood escaped, stuck his finger in the eye of the prostrate man, and then with his open hand slapped him across the face.

"Oh!" gasped Miss Forbes.

The young doctor heard her, and looking up, scowled reprovingly. Seeing she was a rarely beautiful young woman, he scowled less severely; and then deliberately and expertly, again slapped Mr. Jerry Gaylor on the cheek. He watched the white mark made by his hand upon the purple skin, until the blood struggled slowly back to it, and then rose. He ignored every one but the police officer.

"There's nothing the matter with HIM," he said. "He's dead drunk."

The words came to Winthrop with such abrupt relief, bearing so tremendous a burden of gratitude, that his heart seemed to fail him. In his suddenly regained happiness, he unconsciously laughed.

"Are you sure?" he asked eagerly. "I thought I'd killed him."

The surgeon looked at Winthrop coldly. "When they're like that," he explained with authority, "you can't hurt 'em if you throw them off the Times Building."

He condescended to recognize the crowd. "You know where this man lives?"

Voices answered that Mr. Gaylor lived at the corner, over the saloon. The voices showed a lack of sympathy. Old man Gaylor dead was a novelty; old man Gaylor drunk was not.

The doctor's prescription was simple and direct.

"Put him to bed till he sleeps it off," he ordered; he swung himself to the step of the ambulance. "Let him out, Steve," he called. There was the clang of a gong and the rattle of galloping hoofs.

The police officer approached Winthrop. "They tell me Jerry stepped in front of your car; that you wasn't to blame. I'll get their names and where they live. Jerry might try to hold you up for damages."

"Thank you very much," said Winthrop.

With several of Jerry's friends, and the soiled person, who now seemed dissatisfied that Jerry was alive, Winthrop helped to carry him up one flight of stairs and drop him upon a bed.

"In case he needs anything," said Winthrop, and gave several bills to the soiled person, upon whom immediately Gaylor's other friends closed in. "And I'll send my own doctor at once to attend to him."

"You'd better," said the soiled person morosely, "or, he'll try to shake you down."

The opinions as to what might be Mr. Gaylor's next move seemed unanimous.

From the saloon below, Winthrop telephoned to the family doctor, and then rejoined Miss Forbes and the Police officer. The officer gave him the names of those citizens who had witnessed the accident, and in return received Winthrop's card.

"Not that it will go any further," said the officer reassuringly. "They're all saying you acted all right and wanted to take him to Roosevelt. There's many," he added with sententious indignation, "that knock a man down, and then run away without waiting to find out if they've hurted 'em or killed 'em."

The speech for both Winthrop and Miss Forbes was equally embarrassing.

"You don't say?" exclaimed Winthrop nervously. He shook the policeman's hand. The handclasp was apparently satisfactory to that official, for he murmured "Thank you," and stuck something in the lining of his helmet. "Now, then!" Winthrop said briskly to Miss Forbes, "I think we have done all we can. And we'll get away from this place a little faster than the law allows."

Miss Forbes had seated herself in the car, and Winthrop was cranking up, when the same policeman, wearing an anxious countenance, touched him on the arm. "There is a gentleman here," he said, "wants to speak to you." He placed himself between the gentleman and Winthrop and whispered: "He's Izzy Schwab, he's a Harlem police-court lawyer and a Tammany man. He's after something, look out for him."

Winthrop saw, smiling at him ingratiatingly, a slight, slim youth, with beady, rat-like eyes, a low forehead, and a Hebraic nose. He wondered how it had been possible for Jerry Gaylor to so quickly secure counsel. But Mr. Schwab at once undeceived him.

"I'm from the Journal," he began, "not regular on the staff, but I send 'em Harlem items, and the court reporter treats me nice, see! Now about this accident; could you give me the name of the young lady?" He smiled encouragingly at Miss Forbes.

"I could not!" growled Winthrop. "The man wasn't hurt, the policeman will tell you so. It is not of the least public interest."

With a deprecatory shrug, the young man smiled knowingly.

"Well, mebbe not the lady's name," he granted, "but the name of the OTHER gentleman who was with you, when the accident occurred." His black, rat-like eyes snapped. "I think HIS name would be of public interest."

To gain time Winthrop stepped into the driver's seat. He looked at Mr. Schwab steadily. "There was no other gentleman," he said. "Do you mean my chauffeur?"

Mr. Schwab gave an appreciative chuckle. "No, I don't mean your chauffeur," he mimicked. "I mean," he declared theatrically in his best police-court manner, "the man who today is hoping to beat Tammany, Ernest Peabody!"

Winthrop stared at the youth insolently. "I don't understand you," he said.

"Oh, of course not!" jeered Izzy Schwab. He moved excitedly from foot to foot. "Then who WAS the other man," he demanded, "the man who ran away?"

Winthrop felt the blood rise to his face. That Miss Forbes should hear this rat of a man, sneering at the one she was to marry, made him hate Peabody. But he answered easily: "No one ran away. I told my chauffeur to go and call up an ambulance. That was the man you saw."

As when "leading on" a witness to commit himself, Mr. Schwab smiled sympathetically.

"And he hasn't got back yet," he purred, "has he?"

"No, and I'm not going to wait for him," returned Winthrop. He reached for the clutch, but Mr. Schwab jumped directly in front of the car.

"Was he looking for a telephone when he ran up the elevated steps?" he cried. He shook his fists vehemently. "Oh, no, Mr. Winthrop, it won't do- you make a good witness. I wouldn't ask for no better, but, you don't fool Izzy Schwab."

"You're mistaken, I tell you," cried Winthrop desperately. "He may look like- like this man you speak of, but no Peabody was in this car."

Izzy Schwab wrung his hands hysterically.

"No, he wasn't!" he cried, "because he run away! And left an old man in the street- dead, for all he knowed- nor cared neither. Yah!" shrieked the Tammany heeler. "HIM a Reformer, yah!"

"Stand away from my car," shouted Winthrop, "or you'll get hurt."

"Yah, you'd like to, wouldn't you?" returned Mr. Schwab, leaping, nimbly to one side. "What do you think the Journal'll give me for that story, hey? 'Ernest Peabody, the Reformer, Kills an Old Man, AND RUNS AWAY.' And hiding his face, too! I seen him. What do you think that story's worth to Tammany, hey? It's worth twenty thousand votes!" The young man danced in front of the car triumphantly, mockingly, in a frenzy of malice. "Read the extras, that's all," he taunted. "Read 'em in an hour from now!"

Winthrop glared at the shrieking figure with fierce, impotent rage; then, with a look of disgust, he flung the robe off his knees and rose. Mr. Schwab, fearing bodily injury, backed precipitately behind the policeman.

"Come here," commanded Winthrop softly. Mr. Schwab warily approached. "That story," said Winthrop, dropping his voice to a low whisper, "is worth a damn sight more to you than twenty thousand votes. You take a spin with me up Riverside Drive where we can talk. Maybe you and I can 'make a little business.'"

At the words, the face of Mr. Schwab first darkened angrily, and then, lit with such exultation that it appeared as though Winthrop's efforts had only placed Peabody deeper in Mr. Schwab's power. But the rat-like eyes wavered, there was doubt in them, and greed, and, when they turned to observe if any one could have heard the offer, Winthrop felt the trick was his. It was apparent that Mr. Schwab was willing to arbitrate.

He stepped gingerly into the front seat, and as Winthrop leaned over him and tucked and buckled the fur robe around his knees, he could not resist a glance at his friends on the sidewalk. They were grinning with wonder and envy, and as the great car shook itself, and ran easily forward, Mr. Schwab leaned back and carelessly waved his hand. But his mind did not waver from the purpose of his ride. He was not one to be cajoled with fur rugs and glittering brass.

"Well, Mr. Winthrop," he began briskly. "You want to say something? You must be quick-- every minute's money."

"Wait till we're out of the traffic," begged Winthrop anxiously "I don't want to run down any more old men, and I wouldn't for the world have anything happen to you, Mr.--" He paused politely.

"Schwab--Isadore Schwab."

"How did you know MY name?" asked Winthrop.

"The card you gave the police officer"

"I see," said Winthrop. They were silent while the car swept swiftly west, and Mr. Schwab kept thinking that for a young man who was afraid of the traffic, Winthrop was dodging the motor cars, beer vans, and iron pillars, with a dexterity that was criminally reckless.

At that hour Riverside Drive was empty, and after a gasp of relief, Mr. Schwab resumed the attack. "Now, then," he said sharply, "don't go any further. What is this you want to talk about?"

"How much will the Journal give you for this story of yours?" asked Winthrop.

Mr. Schwab smiled mysteriously. "Why?" he asked.

"Because," said Winthrop, "I think I could offer you something better."

"You mean," said the police-court lawyer cautiously, "you will make it worth my while not to tell the truth about what I saw?"

"Exactly," said Winthrop.

"That's all! Stop the car," cried Mr. Schwab. His manner was commanding. It vibrated with triumph. His eyes glistened with wicked satisfaction.

"Stop the car?" demanded Winthrop, "what do you mean?"

"I mean," said Mr. Schwab dramatically, "that I've got you where I want you, thank you. You have killed Peabody dead as a cigar butt! Now I can tell them how his friends tried to bribe me. Why do you think I came in your car? For what money YOU got? Do you think you can stack up your roll against the New York Journal's, or against Tammany's?" His shrill voice rose exultantly. "Why, Tammany ought to make me judge for this! Now, let me down here," he commanded, "and next time, don't think you can take on Izzy Schwab and get away with it."

They were passing Grant's Tomb, and the car was moving at a speed that Mr. Schwab recognized was in excess of the speed limit.

"Do you hear me?" he demanded, "let me down!"

To his dismay Winthrop's answer was in some fashion to so juggle with the shining brass rods that the car flew into greater speed. To Izzy

Schwab it seemed to scorn the earth, to proceed by leaps and jumps. But, what added even more to his mental discomfiture was, that Winthrop should turn, and slowly and familiarly wink at him.

As through the window of an express train, Mr. Schwab saw the white front of Claremont, and beyond it the broad sweep of the Hudson. And, then, without decreasing its speed, the car like a great bird, swept down a hill, shot under a bridge, and into a partly paved street. Mr. Schwab already was two miles from his own bailiwick. His surroundings were unfamiliar. On the one hand were newly erected, untenanted flat houses with the paint still on the window panes, and on the other side, detached villas, a roadhouse, an orphan asylum, a glimpse of the Hudson.

"Let me out," yelled Mr. Schwab, "what you trying to do? Do you think a few blocks'll make any difference to a telephone? You think you're damned smart, don't you? But you won't feel so fresh when I get on the long distance. You let me down," he threatened, "or, I'll..."

With a sickening skidding of wheels, Winthrop whirled the car round a corner and into the Lafayette Boulevard, that for miles runs along the cliff of the Hudson.

"Yes," asked Winthrop, "WHAT will you do?"

On one side was a high steep bank, on the other many trees, and through them below, the river. But there were no houses, and at half-past eight in the morning those who later drive upon the boulevard were still in bed.

"WHAT will you do?" repeated Winthrop.

Miss Forbes, apparently as much interested in Mr. Schwab's answer as Winthrop, leaned forward. Winthrop raised his voice above the whir of flying wheels, the rushing wind and scattering pebbles.

"I asked you into this car," he shouted, "because I meant to keep you in it until I had you where you couldn't do any mischief. I told you I'd give you something better than the Journal would give you, and I am going to give you a happy day in the country. We're now on our way to this lady's house. You are my guest, and you can play golf, and bridge, and the piano, and eat and drink until the polls close, and after that you can go to the devil. If you jump out at this speed, you will break your neck. And, if I have to slow up for anything, and you try to get away, I'll go after you- it doesn't matter where it is- and break every bone in your body."

"Yah! you can't!" shrieked Mr. Schwab. "You can't do it!"

The madness of the flying engines had got upon his nerves. Their poison was surging in his veins. He knew he had only to touch his elbow against the elbow of Winthrop, and he could throw the three of them into eternity. He was traveling on air, uplifted, defiant, carried beyond himself.

"I can't do what?" asked Winthrop.

The words reached Schwab from an immeasurable distance, as from another planet, a calm, humdrum planet on which events moved in commonplace, orderly array. Without a jar, with no transition stage, instead of hurtling through space, Mr. Schwab found himself luxuriously seated in a cushioned chair, motionless, at the side of a steep bank. For a mile before him stretched an empty road. And, beside him in the car, with arms folded calmly on the wheel there glared at him a grim, alert young man.

"I can't do what?" growled the young man.

A feeling of great loneliness fell upon Izzy Schwab. Where were now those officers, who in the police courts were at his beck and call? Where the numbered houses, the passing surface cars, the sweating multitudes of Eighth Avenue? In all the world he was alone, alone on an empty country road, with a grim, alert young man.

"When I asked you how you knew my name," said the young man, "I thought you knew me as having won some races in Florida last winter. This is the car that won. I thought maybe you might have heard of me when I was captain of a football team at-- a university. If you have any idea that you can jump from this car and not be killed, or, that I cannot pound you into a pulp, let me prove to you you're wrong-- now. We're quite alone. Do you wish to get down?"

"No," shrieked Schwab, "I won't!" He turned appealingly to the young lady. "You're a witness," he cried. "If he assaults me, he's liable. I haven't done nothing."

"We're near Yonkers," said the young man, "and if you try to take advantage of my having to go slow through the town, you know now what will happen to you."

Mr. Schwab having instantly planned on reaching Yonkers, to leap from the car into the arms of the village constable, with suspicious alacrity, assented. The young man regarded him doubtfully.

"I'm afraid I'll have to show you," said the young man. He laid two fingers on Mr. Schwab's wrist; looking at him, as he did so, steadily and thoughtfully, like a physician feeling a pulse. Mr. Schwab screamed. When he had seen policemen twist steel nippers on the wrists of prisoners, he had thought, when the prisoners shrieked and writhed, they

She placed her finger on a twisting red line that trickled through a page of type

were acting.

He now knew they were not.

"Now, will you promise?" demanded the grim young man.

"Yes," gasped Mr. Schwab. "I'll sit still. I won't do nothing."

"Good," muttered Winthrop.

A troubled voice that carried to the heart of Schwab a promise of protection, said: "Mr. Schwab, would you be more comfortable back here with me?"

Mr. Schwab turned two terrified eyes in the direction of the voice. He saw the beautiful young lady regarding him kindly, compassionately; with just a suspicion of a smile. Mr. Schwab instantly scrambled to safety over the front seat into the body of the car. Miss Forbes made way for the prisoner beside her and he sank back with a nervous, apologetic sigh. The alert young man was quick to follow the lead of the lady.

"You'll find caps and goggles in the boot, Schwab," he said hospitably. "You had better put them on. We are going rather fast now." He extended a magnificent case of pigskin, that bloomed with fat black cigars. "Try one of these," said the hospitable young man. The emotions that swept Mr. Schwab he found difficult to pursue, but he raised his hat to the lady.

"May I, Miss?" he said.

"Certainly," said the lady.

There was a moment of delay while with fingers that slightly trembled, Mr. Schwab selected an amazing green cap and lit his cigar; and then the car swept forward, singing and humming happily, and scattering the autumn leaves. The young lady leaned toward him with a book in a leather cover. She placed her finger on a twisting red line that trickled through a page of type.

"We're just here," said the young lady, "and we ought to reach home, which is just about there, in an hour."

"I see," said Schwab. But all he saw was a finger in a white glove, and long eyelashes tangled in a gray veil.

For many minutes, or for all Schwab knew, for many miles, the young lady pointed out to him the places along the Hudson, of which he had read in the public school history, and quaint old manor houses set in glorious lawns; and told him who lived in them. Schwab knew the names as belonging to down-town streets, and up-town clubs. He became nervously humble, intensely polite, he felt he was being carried as an honored guest into the very heart of the Four Hundred, and when the car jogged slowly down the main street of Yonkers, although a policeman stood idly within a yard of him, instead of shrieking to him for help, Izzy Schwab looked at him scornfully across the social gulf that separated them, with all the intolerance he believed becoming in the upper classes.

"Those bicycle cops," he said confidentially to Miss Forbes, "are too chesty."

The car turned in between stone pillars, and under an arch of red and golden leaves, and swept up a long avenue to a house of innumerable roofs. It was the grandest house Mr. Schwab had ever entered, and when two young men in striped waistcoats and many brass buttons ran down the stone steps and threw open the door of the car, his heart fluttered between fear and pleasure.

Lounging before an open fire in the hall were a number of young men, who welcomed Winthrop delightedly and, to all of whom Mr. Schwab was formally presented. As he was introduced he held each by the hand and elbow and said impressively, and much to the other's embarrassment, "WHAT name, please?"

Then one of the servants conducted him to a room opening on the hall, from whence he heard stifled exclamations and laughter, and some one saying "Hush." But Izzy Schwab did not care. The slave in brass buttons was proffering him ivory-backed hair-brushes, and obsequiously removing the dust from his coat collar. Mr. Schwab explained to him that he was not dressed for automobiling, as Mr. Winthrop had invited him quite informally. The man was most charmingly sympathetic.

And when he returned to the hall every one received him with the most genial, friendly interest. Would he play golf, or tennis, or pool, or walk over the farm, or just look on? It seemed the wish of each to be his escort. Never had he been so popular.

He said he would "just look on." And so, during the last and decisive day of the "whirlwind" campaign, while in Eighth Avenue voters were being challenged, beaten, and bribed, bonfires were burning, and "extras" were appearing every half hour, Izzy Schwab, the Tammany henchman, with a secret worth twenty thousand votes, sat a prisoner, in a wicker chair, with a drink and a cigar, guarded by four young men in flannels, who played tennis violently at five dollars a corner.

It was always a great day in the life of Izzy Schwab. After a luncheon, which, as he later informed his friends, could not have cost less than "two dollars a plate and drink all you like," Sam Forbes took him on at pool. Mr. Schwab had learned the game in the cellars of Eighth Avenue at two and a half cents a cue, and now, even in Columbus Circle he was a star.

So, before the sun had set, Mr. Forbes, who at pool rather fancied himself, was seventy-five dollars poorer, and Mr. Schwab just that much to the good. Then there followed a strange ceremony called tea, or, if you preferred it, whiskey and soda; and the tall footman bent before him with huge silver salvers laden down with flickering silver lamps, and bubbling soda bottles, and cigars, and cigarettes.

"You could have filled your pockets with twenty-five cent Havanas, and nobody would have said nothing!" declared Mr. Schwab, and his friends who never had enjoyed his chance to study at such close quarters the truly rich, nodded enviously.

At six o'clock Mr. Schwab led Winthrop into the big library and asked for his ticket of leave.

"They'll be counting the votes soon," he begged. "I can't do no harm now, and I don't mean to. I didn't see nothing, and I won't say nothing. But it's election night, and-- and I just GOT to be on Broadway."

"Right," said Winthrop, "I'll have a car take you in, and if you will accept this small check..."

"No!" roared Izzy Schwab. Afterward he wondered how he came to do it. "You've give me a good time, Mr. Winthrop. You've treated me fine, all the gentlemen have treated me nice. I'm not a blackmailer, Mr. Winthrop." Mr. Schwab's voice shook slightly.

"Nonsense, Schwab, you didn't let me finish," said Winthrop, "I'm likely to need a lawyer any time; this is a retaining fee. Suppose I exceed the speed limit-- I'm liable to do that..."

"You bet you are!" exclaimed Mr. Schwab violently.

"Well, then, I'll send for YOU, and there isn't a police magistrate, nor any of the traffic squad, you can't handle, is there?"

Mr. Schwab flushed with pleasure. "You can count on me," he vowed, "and your friends too, and the ladies," he added gallantly. "If ever the ladies want to get bail, tell 'em to telephone for Izzy Schwab. Of course," he said reluctantly, "if it's a retaining fee..."

But when he read the face of the check he exclaimed in protest. "But, Mr. Winthrop, this is more than the Journal would have give me!"

They put him in a car belonging to one of the other men, and all came out on the steps to wave him "good-bye," and he drove magnificently into his own district, where there were over a dozen men who swore he tipped the French chauffeur a five dollar bill "just like it was a cigarette."

All of election day since her arrival in Winthrop's car, Miss Forbes had kept to herself. In the morning, when the other young people were out of doors, she remained in her room, and after luncheon when they gathered round the billiard table, she sent for her cart and drove off alone. The others thought she was concerned over the possible result of the election, and did not want to disturb them by her anxiety. Winthrop, thinking the presence of Schwab embarrassed her, recalling as it did Peabody's unfortunate conduct of the morning, blamed himself for bringing Schwab to the house. But he need not have distressed himself. Miss Forbes was thinking neither of Schwab nor Peabody, nor was she worried or embarrassed. On the contrary, she was completely happy.

When that morning she had seen Peabody running up the steps of the Elevated, all the doubts, the troubles, questions, and misgivings that night and day for the last three months had upset her, fell from her shoulders like the pilgrim's heavy pack. For months she had been telling herself that the unrest she felt when with Peabody was due to her not being able to appreciate the importance of those big affairs in which he was so interested; in which he was so admirable a figure. She had, as she supposed, loved him, because he was earnest, masterful, intent of purpose. His had seemed a fine character. When she had compared him with the amusing boys of her own age, the easy-going joking youths to whom the betterment of New York was of no concern, she had been proud in her choice. She was glad Peabody was ambitious. She was ambitious for him. She was glad to have him consult her on those questions of local government, to listen to his fierce, contemptuous abuse of Tammany. And yet early in their engagement she had missed something, something she had never known, but which she felt sure should exist. Whether she had seen it in the lives of others, or read of it in romances, or whether it was there because it was nature to desire to be loved, she did not know. But long before Winthrop returned from his trip round the world, in her meetings with the man she was to marry, she had begun to find that there was something lacking. And Winthrop had shown her that this something lacking was the one thing needful. When Winthrop had gone abroad he was only one of her brother's several charming friends. One of the amusing merry youths who came and went in the house as freely as Sam himself. Now, after two years' absence, he refused to be placed in that category. He rebelled on the first night of his return. As she came down to the dinner of welcome her brother was giving Winthrop, he stared at her as though she were a ghost, and said, so solemnly that every one in the room, even Peabody, smiled: "Now I know why I came home." That he refused to recognize her engagement to Peabody, that on every occasion he told her, or by some act showed her, he loved her; that he swore she should never marry any one but himself, and that he would never marry any one but her, did not at first, except to annoy, in any way impress her.

But he showed her what in her intercourse with Peabody was lacking. At first she wished Peabody could find time to be as fond of her, as foolishly fond of her, as was Winthrop. But she realized that this was unreasonable. Winthrop was just a hot-headed impressionable boy, Peabody was a man doing a man's work. And then she found that week after week she became more difficult to please. Other things in which she wished Peabody might be more like Winthrop, obtruded themselves. Little things which she was ashamed to notice, but which rankled; and big things, such as consideration for others, and a sense of humor, and not talking of himself. Since this campaign began, at times she had felt that if Peabody said "I" once again, she must scream. She assured herself she was as yet unworthy of him, that her intelligence was weak, that as she grew older and so better able to understand serious affairs, such as the importance of having an honest man at Albany as Lieutenant-Governor, they would become more in sympathy. And now, at a stroke, the whole fabric of self-deception fell from her. It was not that she saw Peabody so differently, but that she saw herself and her own heart, and where it lay. And she knew that "Billy" Winthrop, gentle, joking, selfish only in his love for her, held it in his two strong hands.

For the moment, when as she sat in the car deserted by Peabody this truth flashed upon her, she forgot the man lying injured in the street, the unscrubbed mob crowding about her. She was conscious only that a great weight had been lifted. That her blood was flowing again, leaping, beating, dancing through her body. It seemed as though she could not too quickly tell Winthrop. For both of them she had lost out of their lives many days. She had risked losing him for always. Her only thought was to make up to him and to herself the wasted time.

But throughout the day the one-time welcome, but now intruding, friends and the innumerable conventions of hospitality required her to smile and show an interest, when her heart and mind were crying out the one great fact.

It was after dinner, and the members of the house party were scattered between the billiard-room and the piano. Sam Forbes returned from the telephone.

"Tammany," he announced, "concedes the election of Jerome by forty thousand votes, and that he carries his ticket with him. Ernest Peabody is elected his Lieutenant-Governor by a thousand votes. Ernest," he added, "seems to have had a close call." There was a tremendous chorus of congratulations in the cause of Reform. They drank the health of Peabody. Peabody himself, on the telephone, informed Sam Forbes that a conference of the leaders would prevent his being present with them that evening. The enthusiasm for Reform perceptibly increased.

An hour later Winthrop came over to Beatrice and held out his hand. "I'm going to slip away," he said. "Good-night."

"Going away!" exclaimed Beatrice. Her voice showed such apparently acute concern that Winthrop wondered how the best of women could be so deceitful, even to be polite.

"I promised some men," he stammered, "to drive them down-town to see the crowds."

Beatrice shook her head.

"It's far too late for that," she said. "Tell me the real reason."

Winthrop turned away his eyes.

"Oh! the real reason," he said gravely, "is the same old reason, the one I'm not allowed to talk about. It's cruelly hard when I don't see you," he went on, slowly dragging out the words, "but it's harder when I do; so I'm going to say `good-night' and run into town."

He stood for a moment staring moodily at the floor, and then dropped into a chair beside her.

"And, I believe, I've not told you," he went on, "that on Wednesday I'm running away for good, that is, for a year or two. I've made all the fight I can and I lose, and there is no use in my staying on here to- well- to suffer, that is the plain English of it. So," he continued briskly, "I won't be here for the ceremony, and this is `good-by' as well as `good-night.'"

"Where are you going for a year?" asked Miss Forbes.

Her voice now showed no concern. It even sounded as though she did not take his news seriously, as though as to his movements she was possessed of a knowledge superior to his own. He tried to speak in matter-of-fact tones.

"To Uganda!" he said.

"To Uganda?" repeated Miss Forbes. "Where is Uganda?"

"It is in East Africa; I had bad luck there last trip, but now I know the country better, and I ought to get some good shooting."

Miss Forbes appeared indifferently incredulous. In her eyes there was a look of radiant happiness. It rendered them bewilderingly beautiful.

"On Wednesday," she said. "Won't you come and see us again before you sail for Uganda?"

Winthrop hesitated. "I'll stop in and say good-by to your mother if she's in town, and to thank her. She's been awfully good to me. But you- I really would rather not see you again. You understand, or rather, you don't understand, and," he added vehemently, "you never will understand." He stood looking down at her miserably.

On the driveway outside there was a crunching on the gravel of heavy wheels and an aurora-borealis of lights.

"There's your car," said Miss Forbes. "I'll go out and see you off."

"You're very good," muttered Winthrop. He could not understand. This parting from her was the great moment in his life, and although she must know that, she seemed to be making it unnecessarily hard for him. He had told her he was going to a place very far away, to be gone a long time, and she spoke of saying "good-by" to him as pleasantly as though it was his intention to return from Uganda for breakfast.

Instead of walking through the hall where the others were gathered, she led him out through one of the French windows upon the terrace, and along it to the steps. When she saw the chauffeur standing by the car, she stopped.

"I thought you were going alone," she said.

"I am," answered Winthrop. "It's not Fred; that's Sam's chauffeur; he only brought the car around."

The man handed Winthrop his coat and cap, and left them, and Winthrop seated himself at the wheel. She stood above him on the top step. In the evening gown of lace and silver she looked a part of the moonlight night. For each of them the moment had arrived. Like a swimmer standing on the bank gathering courage for the plunge, Miss Forbes gave a trembling, shivering sigh.

"You're cold," said Winthrop, gently. "You must go in. Good-by."

"It isn't that," said the girl. "Have you an extra coat?"

"It isn't cold enough for..."

"I meant for me," stammered the girl in a frightened voice. "I thought perhaps you would take me a little way, and bring me back."

At first the young man did not answer, but sat staring in front of him, then, he said simply: "It's awfully good of you, Beatrice. I won't forget it."

It was a wonderful autumn night, moonlight, cold, clear and brilliant. She stepped in beside him and wrapped herself in one of his greatcoats. They started swiftly down the avenue of trees.

"No, not fast," begged the girl, "I want to talk to you."

The car checked and rolled forward smoothly, sometimes in deep shadow, sometimes in the soft silver glamour of the moon; beneath them the fallen leaves crackled and rustled under the slow moving wheels. At the highway Winthrop hesitated. It lay before them arched with great and ancient elms; below, the Hudson glittered and rippled in the moonlight.

"Which way do you want to go?" said Winthrop. His voice was very grateful, very humble.

The girl did not answer.

There was a long, long pause.

Then he turned and looked at her and saw her smiling at him with that light in her eyes that never was on land or sea.

"To Uganda," said the girl.

THE END

BRIEF BIOGRAPHIES

RICHARD HARDING DAVIS (1864-1916)

Richard Harding Davis was born on April 18, 1864 in Philadelphia. His father, Lemuel Clarke Davis was an editorial writer on the *Philadelphia Inquirer* and his mother Rebecca Harding Davis was a novelist. With this literary background Davis determined at an early age to become a writer.

College life at Lehigh University and Johns Hopkins University from 1882 to 1886 proved less than successful, but with his father's influence he found a job as a newspaperman at the *Philadelphia Record* in 1886. Davis proved to be a good reporter and landed a job in 1989 with the *New York Sun*. His first major fictional work, *Gallegher and Other Stories* in 1890 led him to assume the position of managing editor of *Harper's Weekly* in 1890.

Davis returned to newspaper reporting in 1895 when he joined William Randolph Hearst's *New York Journal*. He covered the Boer War in Africa and the Greco-Turkish War of 1897. The outbreak of the Spanish American War in 1898 put Davis in the limelight and he quickly rose to become one of the world's leading war correspondents. His stories of the exploits of Theodore Roosevelt and his "Rough Riders" made famous both the future president and the reporter who covered him. His exciting description of the battles of that war, including the Rough Riders' charge up San Juan Hill are still considered the primary source for war historians.

During his years as a war correspondent, Davis continued to write short stories, novels and plays. His most famous novel, *Soldiers of Fortune* (1897) was made into a play and later a movie. He was a prolific writer and at one time three of his plays were running on Broadway while many of his novels were bestsellers. In later years Davis covered the beginnings of World War I and spent his last years raising charitable support for Allied soldiers. Richard Harding Davis died in April, 1916, a week before his fifty-second birthday.

"He was as good an American as ever lived and his heart flamed against cruelty and injustice. His writings form a text-book of Americanism which all our people would do well to read at the present time." *Theodore Roosevelt*

FREDERIC DORR STEELE (1874-1944)

Frederic Dorr Steele was born in a lumber camp near Marquette in Michigan's Upper Peninsula. He grew up in Eagle Mills, Michigan and later in Appleton, Wisconsin. Steele went to New York in 1889, intent on becoming a professional illustrator. He studied at the Art Students League and at the National Academy of Design in New York City and became a prolific illustrator. In 1898, he became a freelance illustrator and he worked for all of the major magazines of his day and is best known for his Sherlock Holmes illustrations beginning in 1903 with *The Return of Sherlock Holmes*. Steele illustrated several books by Richard Harding Davis beginning with the novelette *In The Fog* (1901), and including *The Scarlet Car* (1907) and *Vera, The Medium* (1908).

DEMONTREVILLE PRESS, INC.

P.O. Box 835 ◊ Lake Elmo, Minnesota 55042-0835

U.S.A.

Visit us at:

www.demontrevillepress.com

to find a full range of automotive books!